THE GLASS HEART
(A Collection of Stories... And Such)

Robert Edward Levin

This book is a work of fiction. Places, events, and situations in this story are purely fictional. Any resemblance to actual persons, living or dead, is coincidental.

ISBN: 1-4033-0529-3 (Electronic)
ISBN: 1-4033-0530-7 (Softcover)
ISBN: 1-4033-0531-5 (Hardcover)

This book is printed on acid free paper.

1st Books - rev. 05/23/02

This book is dedicated to my brother Michael, my sister Rona, and the memory of my old friend, Randy Schecter.

For Stacy Lee

O' God
Thy ocean is so great,
and my boat is so small.

Table of Contents:

The Glass Heart

Were they laugh-lines? Jennie wondered as she scrutinized her reflection in the mirror. Or had the last twenty years turned them into creases (not wrinkles, never wrinkles), creases... just as it had turned the five pounds she used to lose on a moment's notice into twenty-five unshakable pounds? Jennie pulled nervously at the curled ends of her silky brown hair, perhaps the last and purest vestige of her youthful beauty and turned away from the mirror... momentarily.

What about the dress? She wondered, looking over her shoulder. Is it too long, too short, too sexy, not sexy enough, or did it, (heaven forbid), make her look fat? The dress was, after all, designed for a tight fit. But how tight is tight? By the same token, how fat is fat? Were her tummy rolls showing? Were her hips sticking out? And did her butt, or for that matter her breasts, once firm images of a high school cheerleader, look as big and as bouncy as they felt?

Jennie took a deep, calming breath (except that it didn't calm her), and turned away from the mirror once more. At least she still had her green eyes – wintergreen is how her mother always described them. Then again, her mother had lousy eyesight. Besides, with the anxiety of her twenty year high school reunion to deprive her of a good night's sleep the entire week, Jennie was more concerned that her eyes looked tired and red. Perhaps her new perfume was the culprit. Perhaps she was allergic to it. And speaking of perfume, what about her makeup? For god sakes what if she put too much on? Worse still, what if she didn't put on enough? Those damn laugh-lines, remember? Or had the last twenty years turned them into creases (not wrinkles, never wrinkles), creases?

Twenty years – hardly a lifetime, and yet, with the reunion a little over an hour away Jennie's thoughts returned to Jeffrey, dear, dear Jeffrey, and she knew that it was also much more than a fading memory.

Jeffrey Marks caught the pitchout in perfect stride, scooted to his left, but seeing no promising daylight reversed directions and headed for the sidelines where, after alluding a couple of would-be tacklers, his speed carried him deep into enemy territory. It was the first time he touched the football all game, and yet, since he wasn't scheduled

1

to play (something about a knee strain, although it really had more to do with skipping a science class the day before), the run was more than he had anticipated. Nevertheless it felt good to be back, good to hear the roar of the Friday night crowd, and good to know that Jennie was cheering him on.

But Jennie always cheered him on...harder and longer than anyone ever had before. From the time they were sophomores and Jeffrey was trying to break into the starting lineup on the varsity football team, through their senior year when Jeffrey was hoping to be offered a football scholarship from any college with a football program.

Yet, for Jennie it wasn't all about the cheering. Sure, it was fun and exciting to have the star running back for a boyfriend, just as it was fun and exciting to stroll down the halls of Avondale High arm-in-arm with one of the cutest (if not the cutest), and most popular boys in school. But Jennie wanted more than just the fun of being the toast of every school party worth attending. Jennie needed more than just the excitement of being every school girl's envy and every school boy's desire. Without something more, in fact, something compelling to separate them from the pack, something wonderful – an intimacy only they would understand, she and Jeffrey would have nothing to build on. Instead, they would likely find themselves trapped in the shallow glamour of their own popularity, or worse, they would become, as Jennie's mother was so fond of saying, "Just a couple of puppy-love candles waiting to be blown out."

So it was...on the warm bed of a foggy September night... moments after Jeffrey had so appropriately declared his everlasting love... that Jennie and Jeffrey became one.

'True love,' that's how she felt from the moment Jeffrey penetrated her virginity, and that's how she explained her unflinching devotion to anyone with a mind to ask – especially her two best friends, who every so often would try and convince her to go out with other people. "You're the prettiest girl in school," they would tout. "You can have any boy you want."

"Maybe so," Jennie would reply. "But why would I want to?"

"Because you're too serious about him," they would respond.

"How can I be too serious about a guy I want to spend the rest of my life with?"

"For starters because you're too young."

"So?"

"So you might find someone better."

"Oh really... like who?" Jennie would ask, often unable to mask the indignation in her voice.

"Someone who doesn't play football."

"What does that mean, someone who doesn't play football? What's wrong with football?"

"Nothing, except that's all he does. He doesn't work, he doesn't study, and he's always going out with his friends."

"What are you guys talking about? We go out all the time."

"Yeah, when he's horny. And only then if you pay your own way."

"That's not true," Jennie would protest. "That's not true at all."

"Yes it is, Jennie, and you need to accept it. Same as you need to accept the fact that he's not good enough for you, that there's somebody out there way better."

"Okay, fine, so maybe Jeffrey's concerned most with Jeffrey," Jennie would concede. "But he's got a lot on his mind. He's got a mother to take care of, he's got to get to college on a football scholarship... he's got a lot on his mind. That doesn't mean he's not good enough. It doesn't make him selfish and irresponsible. It doesn't mean we can't be in love. And it certainly doesn't mean he's not going places, because he is. He says so all the time. All the time."

"God Almighty, it's almost 2002 and they still managed to find me. How n' the hell did that happen?" Jeffrey muttered when he first saw the invitation to his high school reunion sitting atop the stack of bills and other junk mail his mother had been holding for him while he was away.

"How else?" His mother replied. "They sent it in care of me... your landlord, remember? Or have you suddenly decided that that stupid truck you sleep in while you're off gallivantin' between god knows where is home?"

"I wasn't gallivantin' anywhere. I told you, I was interviewing for a job."

Flora Marks, a stocky woman with a stocky voice, stabbed her cigarette until it's smelly, smoldering body stood hunched over in the ashtray, and remarked, "In Clarksville, West Virginia? For two weeks? I doubt it."

"You doubt everything I do, so why should this be any different?"

"That's it, blame it on me," Flora suggested, as she slouched against the unforgiving vinyl kitchen chair and folded her stubby, nicotine-stained fingers in her lap.

"Excuse me," Jeffrey said as he leaned against the kitchen counter, "but aren't you always questioning my motives… or, is that the voice of a little angel I hear ringing in my ears?"

"For someone who needs *my* help to pay *his* bills, you sure are a smart-ass."

Jeffrey smirked. "I get it from you," he replied, the one-time twinkle in his baby blue eyes lost amid years of discontent.

"Like hell," Flora Marks stated. "Like most of your bad habits, you got it from your old man."

"Yeah, it's his fault," Jeffrey responded as he pushed his unkempt black hair into an orderly mess. "He hasn't been around my whole life, but somehow, someway, it's still his fault."

"Think what you want, it happens to be the tru…"

"Go sell it to the milkman."

"Watch your tongue," Flora warned.

"Ooh, big threat, big threat," Jeffrey quipped while his hands did the shimmy.

Flora wheezed in a handful of new air, and said, "Boy, you really don't have respect for nothin' and nobody, do ya?"

"Yeah I do," Jeffrey countered. "I've got the same respect for people that they've got for me."

"Don't know if that's good enough, son."

"Either do I, ma, but it'll have to do 'cuz that's where I am right now."

Flora wrestled the last cigarette from her partially crumpled day-old pack and stuck it between her lips.

"Goin' through those things pretty quick, aren't ya?" Jeffrey asked.

Flora ignored her son's question and fired up.

"What's the matter, you suddenly give up talkin'?"

Flora peeled the cigarette from her mouth, waited until the dirty white smoke collided with the sunlight streaming in through the kitchen window, and replied, "Didn't know you were so concerned about my wellbeing."

Jeffrey walked over to the kitchen table and slumped into a chair across from his mother. "That's a pretty silly thing to say, don't ya think?"

Flora studied the face of her only child, a worn-down, forlorn version of what was once proud and handsome, eager and spirited, vital and strong, and pried loose a reflective smile. "What's happened to you, Jeffrey? What's happened son?" She asked, the delicate tone of her questions quickly easing the tension that had been mounting between them. "Is it me? Have I been that bad of a mother? It wasn't always easy, ya know... what with your father leavin' us for another woman when you were all of two-years-old, havin' to work two jobs, not always bein' there for ya after school. I did the best I could though... I really did."

Jeffrey hung his head and sighed. "It's not you, ma. I wish it were so I'd have someone to blame, but it's not. It's never been. I just can't get nothin' to fall my way. I'm thirty-eight-years-old and no matter how much I try, no matter what I got goin', somethin' always comes along to screw it up. Always."

"I dunno son, maybe you're bein' a bit hard..."

"And ya know the worst part, ma? I've been close... really close... like I could taste it... like it was right in the freakin' palm of my hand."

Jeffrey stood at the bus depot with a suitcase in one hand and a cookie-tin filled with Jennie's homemade cookies in the other. Between the going-away-party thrown by his friends, capped off by a rousing session of sexual intercourse with Jennie, it had been a long night. Still, he was anxious to put it all behind him and pursue his new life at Riley State College, the only school to offer him a football scholarship.

"So what do ya think?" Billy asked, as he and Jeffrey stood underneath the depot awning and watched as light drizzle sprinkled the pavement.

Jeffrey set down his suitcase and glanced at his childhood friend. "About what?"

"You know," Billy replied, his sardonic grin helping to pinpoint the subject matter.

"You mean about Jennie? What about her?"

5

"C'mon Jeffrey, don't hand me that. You know what I'm talkin' about. How'd ya leave it with her?"

Jeffrey arched his eyebrows and flashed a sardonic grin of his own. "I didn't. I just sorta told her that once I got settled in I'd send her a bus ticket and she could come up for a visit. Luckily she'll be startin' nursing school soon so who knows if she'll even have the time."

"So are ya sorta gonna?" Billy asked, the curious look in his small brown eyes somehow minimized by the fleshy roundness of his face.

"What, send her a ticket? And give up all those college babes? Are you nuts? Hell, I'll call her a few times, drop her a letter or two, but that's it. High school's over...know what I mean?" Jeffrey responded.

"Yeah, I know what you mean. I just wanted to make sure you weren't goin' off the deep end with her."

Jeffrey winked. "Trust me bud. The thought never crossed my mind."

Riley State College, though only a few hundred miles north of Avondale often experienced the kind of weather (specifically heavy rains and cold blustery winds, which either turned the football field into a wading pool, or a frozen tundra), that made running a football difficult; particularly for someone like Jeffrey who did not enjoy head-down, ass-up, straight away, smash-mouth football, but rather, preferred to rely on his speed and a handful of shake-and-bake-moves to allude would-be tacklers. Nevertheless, Jeffrey never gave the weather or his running style a second thought until Coach Billingham stood before the team after a lackadaisical practice one afternoon, and barked, "Marks, get your fanny up here!"

"What's up Coach? What do ya need?" Jeffrey asked, as he sauntered to the front of the room in his football pants and semi-sweaty tee shirt.

Coach Billingham pulled the cigar-stub from his mouth, and snapped, "What I need is for you to stand there and keep your big trap shut."

"Sure Coach, whatever you say."

6

Coach Billingham circled Jeffrey, and after scanning him from top to bottom, his eyes squinting as though half-blinded by the sun, asked, "How tall are you son? How tall?"

"Six-foot-one," Jeffrey replied casually.

"Uh-huh, and how much do ya weigh son? How much?"

Jeffrey flashed his teammates a bewildered look, before replying, "I dunno... two-ten, two-twenty. Why, what's up?"

"Six-one and roughly two-hundred and fifteen pounds – is that what you're tellin' me?"

Jeffrey shrugged his broad shoulders. "Yeah, I guess," he replied with a nervous smile.

Coach Billingham rested his fingers on the shelves of his overflowing gut and moved a few paces away, leaving Jeffrey center stage. "Well since you're one of the few football players I've met in my life who doesn't know his precise weight, I can only guess. So am I right, is two-hundred and fifteen pounds an accurate guess? Yes or no?"

"Yes."

"Okay, so you're six-one, two-fifteen... correct?"

"Yes Coach, that's correct," Jeffrey replied, the furrow of his brow accenting the sudden rigidity in his voice.

"Good – now that we've got that settled I want everybody to listen up. I want y'all payin' very close attention to what I'm about to say." Coach Billingham dipped his bald-head toward Jeffrey. "Men, the first time I ever saw Marks here play football I was impressed. In fact, I was quite impressed. Figured there'd be ten, maybe fifteen schools lookin' to give him a scholarship. And why not?" Coach Billingham asked, as he shrugged his round, sloping shoulders. "He's got great size for a running-back, good hands, and good speed. On top of all that he sees the field pretty doggone well too. That's why I couldn't understand it when no other colleges recruited him. No way the good Lord's lettin' this boy slip through the cracks, all the way to me, I said to myself. Too good to be true, I figured. But now, after watchin' him lollygag through more practices than I care to admit, I've come to understand what every other college recruiter must've already known." Coach Billingham extended his arm, and said, "Men, I give you Jeffrey Marks – a man with all the physical tools to play this game, but... but... who does not possess the two things he needs most to be successful. One is desire. The other is heart. Now," Coach

7

Billingham added, holding up his palm as if to quiet a wildly cheering crowd, "before y'all start thinking that I'm being too hard on Mr. Marks here, let me assure you that I am not. The truth is I've already had this conversation with him. Twice, in fact. But evidently everything I said went in one ear and out the other, so I thought it best to bring it before the team. Not to embarrass him, to help him understand that it affects everybody anytime an individual doesn't pull his own weight. The team comes first – knowing it makes you a better football player – acting like it makes you a better man. The problem I have, the problem we all have is that right now Mr. Marks isn't willing to work, he isn't willing to charge forward, he isn't willing to sacrifice. What he is willing to do is blame the weather and his teammates for his screw-ups and shoddy play. And we can't have that here, can we?" Coach Billingham asked, while scouring the subdued faces of his football players. "No gentlemen, we can't. However...however...in order to be fair to Mr. Marks, I am prepared to give him another chance. But it won't be at running-back. It'll be as a member of the special teams... kickoffs and punt returns. And, and," Coach Billingham added, once again flashing his palm as if to quiet a wildly cheering crowd, "if Mr. Marks decides to work like the rest of us – if he shows me that he's willing to give the necessary effort – if he's prepared to look only at himself whenever he comes up short then I will give him another crack at running-back." Coach Billingham glanced at Jeffrey. "Understood, Mr. Marks?"

Jeffrey stared at his feet and did not respond, prompting Coach Billingham to let him dangle in a long and naked moment of silence, before concluding, "As for the rest of you, remember this – Mr. Marks is merely an example of what you can all expect anytime I sense another player who's willing to talk the talk, but not walk the walk. Understood?" Coach Billingham asked, once again scouring the subdued faces of his football team. "Good, then get showered and I'll see you all back here tomorrow."

"Kickoffs and punt returns? What the hell is that?" Jeffrey asked his roommate later that evening.

Willie Bean, a mammoth offensive tackle, shrugged his sprawling shoulders, causing his neck to momentarily disappear, and said, "Hey, he's looking to make an example out of you b'cuz he thinks you got lots of ability. He's tryin' to goad you into gettin' the most out of it, that's all. Hell, it ain't like he's taking away your scholarship and tossin' you out of school."

"Bullshit," Jeffrey said, as he walked over to the closet and scanned his small collection of shirts. "Special teams are for kamikazes and I'm a running-back for Christ's sake. Even my high school coach didn't make me play special teams."

"Yeah, but this ain't high school ball. This is college, where everybody's bigger, faster and tougher, and all you can hope for is an opportunity to keep up wherever they play ya. Besides, if you're half the athlete you're always sayin' you are then it shouldn't be no problem, should it?" Willie cracked.

"Aw what the hell do you know, you're a goddamn lineman for cryin' out loud."

Willie cupped his thick hands behind his thick head and leaned against that portion of the dorm-room wall which served as his bed's headboard. "I know that your old high school sweetie called," he said with a snicker.

"Jennie... again? Christ, I just wrote her a fuckin' letter a week ago."

"Guess she wants to talk to ya."

"Yeah, well I can't afford long distance," Jeffrey replied, as he discarded the shirt he was holding and reached for a sweater instead. "Scholarship money don't cover it... know what I mean?"

"Don't give me that roomie. You're just afraid she's gonna make you feel guilty for actin' like she don't exist."

"Hardly," Jeffrey said, his assertion muted by the sweater he was pulling over his head.

"Hardly my ass," Willie countered.

"Okay, hardly your ass," Jeffrey sneered. "Meanwhile, what'd she say?"

"Is my honeybunch there?" Willie cooed, his dimples the size of quarters. "Oh where oh where is my scrumptious, lovey-dovey, honeybunch?"

"So you didn't tell her nothin'... right?" Jeffrey asked, his effortless good looks obscured by a moment of trepidation.

"No I didn't tell her nothin'. But I think you should... as in you ain't interested no more," Willie responded. "Christ, for six weeks now all she's done is write letters and call, and all you do is ignore her."

Jeffrey caught the large, unsympathetic face of his roommate staring at him while he stood in front of the mirror, and said, "First of all I thought she'd get the message by now so don't give me any shit just b'cuz she hasn't. Second of all I told you, I mailed her a letter last week so don't act like I'm bein' all hard about it. And third of all, who the hell are you anyway, a big, ugly version of Ann Landers?"

"First of all, fuck you," Willie shot back, his square jaw tightening, in turn drawing his eyebrows close to the bridge of his twice-broken nose. "Second of all, fuck you. And third of all, I can't wait to see you run after her the moment they throw you out of this place. I only hope she's got herself a new squeeze by then and don't give a rat's-ass about you."

"Yeah? Well get this buddy...no one's throwin' me out of anywhere, so it doesn't really matter."

"Whatever you say," Willie uttered the moment Jeffrey stormed out of the room. "Whatever you say."

As a city, Riley, Indiana, was slow in achieving the status that Hayden Riley envisioned for it when he first stood on the county courthouse steps well over a century ago and proclaimed Riley, "A small town today, a city of lights tomorrow!" In fact, it wasn't until Hayden grew terminally ill (an inevitable occurrence since he regularly doused his bleeding ulcer with Bloody Marys), that the square mile of land he'd spent years accumulating actually evolved into something besides a testimonial to himself.

Like his father, Hayden Jr., a savvy, if not altogether crooked lawyer, also saw Riley as much more than a vast and rolling farmland. Yet, unlike his father, Hayden Jr. realized that with a little more planning and a lot less drinking he might also see Riley become, not just a thriving enterprise, but a gateway city to the twentieth century; a prospect that would require the railroad – a surefire way to introduce people with money to goods and services.

At the time, however, the Midwest Railway Company was already committed to laying tracks and building a train station some thirty miles north of Riley. Still, Hayden Jr. was nothing if not persuasive. A bribe here, a payoff there – a promise one day, a lie the next – a smalltime swindle, a big-time scam – "The greater the need," as Hayden Jr. was so fond of pontificating, "the bigger the deed." Big enough, in fact, that within a few years Hayden Jr. saw his dreams

10

materialize, for the railway system was not only in place, it brought the bountiful increase in population, property values, and overall development that Hayden Jr. had hoped for. A dress store here, a haberdashery there – a hotel on one corner, a grocery store on the other – a restaurant in the middle of the street, a stoplight at the end of it. Soon, it was only a matter of time before Riley, Indiana, grew from a single square mile to more than half-a-dozen, its rapid growth culminating in plans to begin construction on a small college before the end of 1930.

Unfortunately Hayden Jr. did not live to see the school's completion. He died in the psychiatric ward of Riley City Hospital in 1932, a syphilitic and gonorrheal wreck. Fortunately he was survived by his able son, Hayden Riley III. A Yale graduate with a keen mind, a steady hand and a dangerous thirst to command, not to mention an ego the size of the St. Lawrence River, Hayden III did more than carry on his father's legacy. He bulldozed his way into new housing markets, renovated and expanded retail districts, developed the city's first industrial center, and increased the size of the university, the student body and the attendant entertainment dollar...via the new football stadium, aptly named, Hayden Riley Stadium.

Regardless of his consuming work schedule, however, Hayden Riley III managed to find time to marry... three different women. His first wife lasted some eight months, leaving him while he was at work one day because she could no longer absorb his punishing demands, particularly the abusive nature of his late night sexual desires. His second wife faired somewhat better, coaxing two years out of her life simply because she was too drunk with her opulent lifestyle to walk away any sooner. His third wife, Alicia, a domineering personality in her own right not only stayed married to Hayden III, notwithstanding the often volatile nature of their relationship, she gave him a son, Hayden Riley IV.

And just like his father before him, Hayden Riley IV was determined to pound his way into the annals of Riley, Indiana history. He did too... though not until he silenced his father's longtime and steadfast declaration, "You're under my thumb boy, remember that!"

It was a cold and blustery January night. Yet, despite the wretched weather, the eight inches of snow blowing relentlessly from one corner of the city to the other, the icy roads choking back traffic and the downed electrical lines rendering portions of the city powerless, despite every local news station warning of no letup in sight, Hayden Riley IV's birthday celebration went on without a hitch. Of course since his mother and father were making the party, with virtually every invited guest a business associate of his father, Hayden IV was not the least bit surprised the lavish home of his parents was streaming with people.

Nevertheless, Hayden IV spent half the evening either watching his young son, Hayden Riley V, sleep in one of the six guest bedrooms, or trying to steady the tattered nerves of his amphetamine addicted wife, Ariel. He did, however, spend the other half of the evening mingling with the stuffy crowd, the stiff conversation and the stale cigar smoke, drinking vodka martinis. The martinis... they were damn good, too. Good to the last spanking drop good. So good, in fact, so cuddly warm, so silky smooth, and so fuck-you righteous, that when midnight rolled around and his father strolled to the front of the main dining room like the Captain of Industry he was, and barked, "Boy, get on up here and show these fine folk how to light a birthday cake," Hayden IV hurled his empty martini glass to the imported Italian marble floor, and barked back, "Damn-it, I'm not a boy. And I'm certainly not your boy. I'm thirty-five years old. Get it!?"

Hayden III glared at his son, his simmering focus dismissing the presence of the startled faces standing between them, and snapped, "What I get is that you're a pathetic little drunk who needs to be tucked into bed right now."

"What you get," Hayden IV countered, his tone rising at the speed of his swelling chest, "is what you created. And if you don't like what you see then the hell with you!"

Hayden III held out his champagne flute until one of the half-dozen servants rushed it from his hand, and then marched forward, his guests parting as he moved to the center of the room, where he stopped, exhaled a large dose of disgust, and said, "I want every person in this room to look at my son. I want you all to see what I've had to endure ever since he graduated college – with a master's degree in economics no less. A master's degree in economics... what and the hell are you going to do with that? I once asked him. You gonna work for me? You gonna take over some day? You gonna be king, is that it? Are those your plans?" Hayden Riley III shook his head and snickered. "Yeah, those are his plans alright – only I do all the work and he does all the drinking. Hell people, my kid couldn't

12

run around the block, let alone run a business empire like mine. He knows it too... knows it because I tell him. He just refuses to hear the truth, that's all. He'd rather spend his time getting drunk, but look at him, just look at him... he can't even do that like a man. No boy, you may have turned thirty-five today, but to me, you're nothing but a sniveling punk inside a man's body. In fact," Hayden III added, as he turned away, "it sickens me to have to look at you."

"Don't turn your back on me, you son-of-a-bitch," Hayden IV warned.

Hayden III stopped dead in his tracks, before slowly, dramatically, turning to face his son once again. "What did you say?"

"I said don't turn your back on me, you rotten son-of-a-bitch."

Hayden III shifted his weight to the heels of his feet, folded his arms, and growled, "Or what?"

Hayden IV stared at his father. Just stared. He could no longer glue the pieces of his shattered spirit together – no longer soothe the pain of his broken heart – no longer breathe the air of his father's dark and confining shadow – no longer stand in the skin of his oft reminded failures – and no longer calm the rage of his deeply rooted hatred, for when his father took a step toward him and growled once again, "Or what boy? I said, or what?" Hayden IV rushed him like the freight train out of control he was.

Hayden III tried to brace himself for the impact, but since his son's charge was so quick, so unexpected, and so overpowering to a man his age, he could not.

Hayden III crashed to the floor hard, very hard. But Hayden IV cared not. Rather, he grabbed his father's head and smashed it against the marble over and over; stopping only after he could no longer fight off the arms trying to pull him off his father's body; though it no longer mattered... his father was dead.

Hayden IV was placed in a mental institution, where he died of heart failure on the eve of his thirty-sixth birthday. His wife, Ariel, faired no better. She died of an overdose soon after her husband was buried, leaving Hayden Riley V to be raised in the cradle of his domineering, but very wealthy grandmother.

Jeffrey Marks climbed aboard the same barstool he'd been parking his ass in ever since the football season began six weeks earlier and ordered a beer. The bar was quiet, almost empty, in fact, except for another student having a drink a couple of stools away; a lean, almost scrawny sort, although he was well dressed and as finely manicured as a guy could be without looking like he came straight from the pages of a magazine. Jeffrey nodded, but the student simply stared at him in return. Jeffrey didn't think much of it until he downed half his beer and realized the student was still gawking at him. "What?" Jeffrey finally asked, annoyed.

"You're on the football team, aren't ya?" The student asked, his voice somewhat deeper than Jeffrey would've guessed.

"Yep," Jeffrey returned, as he hoisted his glass. "I'm on the big bad football team."

"I've seen you play," the student offered, along with a friendly smile.

Jeffrey helped himself to a healthy swallow of beer then set his mug back on the counter. "You want a medal or somethin'?"

"Don't get much playing time, do ya?"

"Hey pal, why don't you buzz off," Jeffrey snapped.

"Whoa, whoa, whoa," the student said, tossing his hand into the air. "I didn't mean anything by what I said. It was just an observation. Sorry if I offended you."

Jeffrey turned in his stool. Straight on the student didn't look as thin as his profile otherwise appeared. Still, between his high cheekbones, small, slightly turned-up nose, and the anxious look that seemed stuck in his eyes, he wasn't going to scare anybody anytime soon. "Buy me a beer and I won't be offended," Jeffrey replied casually.

"You got it. Mike, get my friend a beer," the student promptly called out to the bartender.

"Sure thing Hayden," the bartender called back.

Jeffrey reached for his beer mug. "Name's Hayden, eh?" He asked, without the least bit of interest.

"Yeah... Hayden Riley."

Jeffrey stopped short of bringing the beer mug to his mouth, though he held it in front of his face for a couple of moments before lowering it back to the counter. "Hayden Riley as in the football stadium, Hayden Riley?" He asked, his tone caught somewhere between surprise and disbelief.

Hayden shrugged his shoulders and offered Jeffrey a sheepish grin.

"You're kidding, right?" Jeffrey asked.

Hayden shook his head. "Afraid not," he said.

"No really, you are kidding," Jeffrey asserted.

"No really, I'm not. I never kid... not about that."

"No shit," Jeffrey muttered, as he ingested the unexpected reality. "No shit."

"But you can call me Five," Hayden quickly volunteered. "Everybody calls me Five... everybody except my grandmother." Hayden crinkled up his nose, and added, "She doesn't like the sound of it. Not dignified enough."

"Why Five?"

Hayden smiled. "Because I'm the fifth Hayden Riley."

Jeffrey waited until the bartender delivered his new chilled mug of beer then pulled it from the counter and held it up for a toast. "My name's Jeffrey Marks. But you can call me Jeffrey," he cracked.

Hayden nodded. "I know, you're the running back from Avondale."

"Wrong, I used to be a running back. Now I play on special teams. How'd you know me anyway?"

Hayden shrugged his shoulders and offered Jeffrey another sheepish grin. "I saw your picture in this year's football program. Plus I read your bio. But don't worry, I read everyone's bio, not just yours."

"Football fan, eh?" Jeffrey queried.

"Probably not as big a fan as you, but sure, I like it."

"Well Five, I hate to break it to ya, but lately I'm not much of a fan at all."

Hayden skimmed his White Russian, decided it had been properly mixed, and then gazed at Jeffrey, and asked, "Really, how come?"

"Because I'm playin' for a coach who likes nothin' more than to ride my ass. And frankly it gets real tiring."

"But isn't that the way team sports go sometimes?" Hayden asked earnestly.

"Maybe, although it's not somethin' I've ever had to deal with before," Jeffrey replied, before draining a quarter of his beer.

"Yeah, but maybe that's one of the differences between high school and college," Hayden proffered.

Jeffrey wiped his beer froth moustache with the back of his hand, and then said, "All I know is that I was a great athlete when I came here. Did I suddenly get bad? Is that what I'm supposed to believe just because I play for a coach who either can't recognize my talent or doesn't know how to utilize it?"

Hayden stood up and leaned his bony ribcage against the bar. "Well, being that I've never played an organized sport in my life, it's not something I should answer."

"Meaning what?" Jeffrey asked.

"Meaning I'm probably not the most qualified person to answer, that's all."

"Okay, that's fair, I suppose," Jeffrey said, dipping his head from side to side. "But then tell me this, Five... have you ever had to do something you didn't want to?"

Hayden's body jumped forward as he gagged up the milky White Russian he had just swallowed.

"Something I said?" Jeffrey asked snickering.

Hayden Riley V quickly grabbed a napkin and dabbed the corners of his mouth. It was another couple of seconds, however, before his body steadied, the water in his eyes dried, and he was able to say, "You mean, other than having to go to college here?"

"Why, you didn't wanna go here?" Jeffrey asked, his wry grin quickly fading.

"No, I wanted to go somewhere out of state, but since my grandmother calls the shots my options were limited. So yes, in answer to your question, I've done things I've not wanted to. It comes with being in my family. The school thing, that's just a small example."

"Well I'm not sure I'm cut out for doing things I don't want to," Jeffrey asserted.

"Guess you just have to weigh your options then," Hayden responded. "I mean, in my case there are some obvious benefits to going along with my grandmother, so while I may not always like them, I do them because it's better than upsetting the apple cart."

"Hey listen, if I had your money I'd do the same thing," Jeffrey stated. "In fact, why go to school at all? Why not just go work for the family? Hell, you're probably going to anyway."

Hayden Riley V smiled at Jeffrey's sneering envy, and said, "Those are my options. What are yours?"

Jeffrey did not respond until he finished off his beer, set down the empty mug (hard), and said, "I guess I can always quit. Take the rest of this year off, get a job, then go to another college where I have a chance to try out. Then, after I make the team, which I will, they'll offer me a scholarship and just like that I'm back in business."

"Just like that, huh?"

"Yep," Jeffrey declared, "just like that."

"Sounds like you've got it all worked out."

"Hey, it's either that or I wait around until my asshole of a coach decides to play me where I'm supposed to play... and I don't feel like waiting around. I didn't come here for that. I didn't come here to waste time."

"Say Mike?" Hayden suddenly called out, "Can we get a couple more drinks here? You want one right?" He asked, glancing at Jeffrey.

"Long as you're buyin', I'm drinkin'", Jeffrey replied.

Hayden Riley V rubbed the smoothness of his cheeks for a moment or two, before asking, "So what's stopping you... about leaving, I mean?"

"Nothin'. I've been thinking about it the last couple of weeks. Ever since I realized that my coach wasn't man enough to keep his word about moving me back to running back if I busted my tail... which I have since he first challenged me. All I'm really waitin' on is to find out if my friend's cousin can get me a job where he's working. If he can, there's a good chance I'll leave."

"What kind of job?"

"He works construction for some big outfit in town." Jeffrey paused while Mike the bartender set down his beer, whereupon he quickly retrieved it from the counter, held it up, and said, "Here's to ya."

Hayden Riley V skimmed his White Russian, decided it had been properly mixed, and then countered, "No, no, here's to you."

"Anyway," Jeffrey continued, "I'm not much of a construction guy, but Larry, that's my friend's cousin, he says they can always use a strong back to do labor. He's gonna put me up too. He's got a finished basement – says I can stay there till I get my feet on the ground. Of course, you probably don't know much about sleeping in finished basements, do ya, Five?"

"*I don't know much about construction either,*" *Hayden quipped,* "*but that hasn't prevented my family from owning the only big construction outfit around these parts.*"

Jeffrey rolled his eyes before casting them on the stained glass mirror behind the bar. "*So if I get this job I'll be working for your family's company, is that what you're tellin' me?*"

Hayden grinned.

"*Must be nice to be you,*" *Jeffrey muttered, as though contemplating the possibilities.*

"*Like most things, it has its moments,*" *Hayden confessed.* "*Good and bad.*"

"*Yeah, well anytime you wanna trade places you be sure to let me know,*" *Jeffrey said, as he turned and looked Hayden square in the eyes.*

"*Not until I find out just how nice that basement is,*" *Hayden joked.*

Jeffrey stared at Hayden for a moment, and then abruptly shook his head, and said, "*Ya know, Five, you're alright for a rich kid... you're alright.*"

"*Ah yessss,*" *Hayden said in his best W.C. Fields impersonation,* "*the issue of the rich kid lives againnnn. Ah yessss.*"

"*What the hell are you talking about?*" *Jeffrey asked, his expression a twisted mess as one eyebrow reached for his hairline while the other one hung tight to the wrinkled bridge of his nose.*

"*Nothing, forget it,*" *Hayden instructed.*

"*Forget nothing, what the hell did you mean?*"

Hayden sighed, but otherwise remained silent.

"*Hey, c'mon Five, that ain't fair. Tell me what you meant,*" *Jeffrey implored.* "*I'm curious. I really...*"

"*The rich kid,*" *Hayden broke in.* "*I'm okay for a rich kid. Everywhere I go, I'm a rich kid. Not just a kid or student, not just somebody's friend or boyfriend... but a rich kid, a rich student, a rich friend, a rich boyfriend.*" *Hayden paused, before adding,* "*It takes the regular out of it... know what I mean?*"

"*Sounds to me like I hit a sore spot,*" *Jeffrey suggested, before throwing down a mouthful of beer.*

"*Maybe, but that doesn't mean it's not the truth.*"

"Why, all your friends your friends because you come from money – same as with all your girlfriends?" Jeffrey fashioned himself a wry grin. "You do go out with girls, don't you, Five?"

"Boy, you really don't want that construction job, do you?" Hayden countered.

"Pulling the power trip are ya?"

"Nah, I'm just having some fun with ya," Hayden replied. "And just so ya know, I do go out with girls. One in particular."

"Really now, what's her name?"

"Rebecca... Rebecca Graham."

"Good lookin'?" Jeffrey asked, before diving into his beer mug once again.

Hayden swirled a straw through his drink, and said, "No, she's not good looking, she's flat out beautiful."

"How long you been seein' her?"

"A little over a year. We're supposed to get married after I graduate this spring."

"This spring?"

"Yep, this spring."

"So you're a senior then, yes?" Jeffrey asked.

"No, I'm really a junior, but I skipped a year." Hayden shrugged his shoulders and offered Jeffrey another sheepish grin. "I guess I'm kind of smart."

Jeffrey sighed, and then said, "Rich, smart, and a good lookin' girl to boot. Not bad, Five. Still, don't ya think you're a little young to be getting married?"

"Maybe, but if I know she's the right one, what's the difference?"

"Nothin', I guess, as long as it's okay with your grandmother."

"Actually my grandmother likes her quite a lot," Hayden said, before swallowing Jeffrey's sarcasm down with a dose of White Russian.

"Well good, then I'm happy for ya, Five."

Hayden set his glass on the counter and winked at Jeffrey. "And she doesn't like many people."

Jeffrey held up his beer mug. "Like I said, I'm happy for ya."

"Well thanks, that's real kind of you to say. But now, what about you – any girlfriends?"

"Not lately," Jeffrey replied. "Had one back in Avondale though. Name's Jennie. She's good lookin' too."

"*So what happened?*"

"*Nothin' really. I mean, once I got the scholarship up here I decided a girlfriend wasn't what I wanted. Too many college babes to check out, know what I'm sayin'?*" *Jeffrey asked, his blue eyes shimmering.*

"*And have you been checking any out?*" *Hayden queried, his brown eyes shimmering in return.*

"*Yeah, I've rolled around with one or two.*"

"*So then this girl, Jennie, she's out of the picture for good?*"

"*Sounds to me like a beer question, Five.*"

Hayden smiled, and then promptly turned and instructed Mike to put another beer on his tab.

"*Thanks,*" *Jeffrey said.*

"*No problem. I'm rich, remember?*"

"*Shit, I'd do the same for you if I could afford it.*"

"*I'm sure you would,*" *Hayden remarked.* "*But that's not important. I'm more interested in this old girlfriend of yours back home. For instance, how'd ya leave it with her?*"

Jeffrey shook his head. "*I didn't... not really, anyway. I just told her that once I got settled I'd send her a bus ticket and she could come up for a visit.*"

"*So let me guess, the bus ticket never got mailed.*"

"*Boy, you are smart, aren't ya?*" *Jeffrey cracked.*

"*Hey, I've got to keep up with my company, don't I?*" *Hayden countered.*

"*Very funny,*" *Jeffrey replied, his derisive grin exposing a hint of eyeteeth.* "*Meanwhile, no, the bus ticket never got mailed. Instead we've traded letters. She's sent me something like twenty-six, and I've sent her three... no, make that four.*"

"*No phone calls?*"

Jeffrey moved his arms away from the counter so Mike the bartender could set down his beer. "*Sure, plenty of phone calls. At last count she was up to forty-seven of 'em.*"

"*But you, you never call her?*"

Jeffrey hoisted his beer from the bar. "*Hell no, I try to avoid talking to her altogether. All she's gonna do is repeat what's in her letters. You know, I love you, I miss you, where are you, all that sort of gooey-hooey.*"

Hayden swirled a straw through his drink, and asked, *"So, how long did you see her back home?"*

"All three years of high school."

"Long time."

"Yeah, we started seeing each other just before her father died. And once he was gone all she had left was her mother and me. There was no other family anywhere. So, I kinda became the man in her world, even though I was all of sixteen. Anyway she grew real dependent on me, I mean real dependent, which is why I think she's so afraid to lose me now. In a weird way I sometimes think that for her, losing me is like losing her father all over again. Does that make sense?" Jeffrey asked, before making love to his beer.

"Sure, it makes a lot of sense," Hayden mused. *"It's sad, too."*

"But hey, life goes on, doesn't it, Five?"

Hayden stared at Jeffrey for what seemed like a weightless moment in time and space, before he abruptly shook his head, and said, *"Hey, speaking of that, I've got an appointment to keep, so I've got to go. But listen, don't worry about that job, Jeffrey. I'll put in a word for ya tomorrow."*

"A good word, or a bad word?"

Hayden winked. *"Far be it from me to hold you back. In fact, I'm going to make sure they pay you more than they normally would. It'll give you a chance to get wherever you're going a whole lot faster."*

"That's great, thanks," Jeffrey replied as he shook Hayden's hand. *"Thanks for the beer, too. You're alright, man... you're alright."*

Hayden smiled then walked to the door, where outside in the chilly night air, he muttered, *"You mean, for a rich kid, don't ya Jeffrey?"*

Jeffrey Marks never thought he'd be going to Hayden Riley's twenty-first birthday party, but when Larry's sister, Maxine, approached him about going as her date (she and Hayden's fiancé were sorority sisters), that's precisely what took place.

Still, when Jeffrey told Larry of the news, Larry's initial reaction was, *"Hey, I was happy to help you get that construction gig. And I'm more than happy to put you up in my basement – what's it been, two, two-and-a-half-months now? But that don't mean I'm throwin' my sister into the deal."*

21

"Look man," Jeffrey responded, "me n' your sister are just goin' as friends, so there's no need for you to worry about her fringe benefits, if you know what I mean."

"She likes you though, Jeffrey... a lot. And I know b'cuz it ain't very often that she asks someone out on a date."

"Larry, Larry, Larry, you ain't thinkin' this through," Jeffrey insisted. "I'm goin' with your sister for free eats and drinks, and that's it. No one's gonna do anything wrong. I promise. Besides, it'll get me out of the house for a change – and let's face it, ever since I quit the football team the chicks haven't been lining up to take me out."

"Yeah, I know, that's one of the reasons I'm not thrilled with the idea. I figure you might have a little pressure buildin' up."

"C'mon man, give me a little more credit than that. It's your sister for Christ sakes."

"I would if I thought you deserve it."

"Look it," Jeffrey said, rolling his eyes impatiently, "you know how I always tell you that I hate fat chicks?"

"Yeah, so?" Larry asked.

"So your sister, Maxine..."

"What about her?"

"Well... she's a fat chick, okay?" Jeffrey replied, his words marching out in nonchalant fashion. "She's a fat chick. Feel better now?"

"Oh yeah," Larry answered, "that makes me feel great... real great."

"Larry," Jeffrey said, waving his hands as though wiping the verbal-slate clean, "that didn't come out right. I only meant that I'm not interested in Maxine that way. It doesn't matter how much I wanna get laid, okay? It won't change anything."

"Ya know," Larry said, shaking his head in disgust, "my sister may be fat, but you Jeffrey, you're a pig."

Jeffrey manufactured a good ol' hometown smile. "Yeah, but I'm harmless," he replied, and then proceeded to skew his eyebrows heavenward.

"You better be," Larry suggested, though his warning rode out on the tail of a long and apprehensive sigh.

The party was called for eight o'clock sharp and by the time Maxine and Jeffrey arrived in Maxine's year-old Camry, the place *was buzzing with life. Quite the place it was, too. Not the lavish estate of Hayden's grandmother, but a guesthouse located on the same sprawling acreage – well now – that wasn't too shabby for a kid; or, as Jeffrey said to Maxine just before they entered the house through a pair of nine-foot doors, "Not too shabby for a rich kid."*

Hayden Riley V was knee deep in partygoers, but when he saw Jeffrey floating through the crowd like a kid at his first circus he quickly maneuvered his way toward him, smiling as though he had just seen an old friend. "Hey Jeffrey," he called out, his hand waving above a swarm of bouncing heads.

"Hey Five, how ya doin'?" Jeffrey called back, and then extended his hand and waited for Hayden to take hold of it.

"You look lost," Hayden declared.

"Man, this is quite the place, Five."

Hayden shot a quick glance around the crowded room and shrugged. "Yeah, not bad, I guess."

"How many people you got here anyway?" Jeffrey asked.

"I dunno… about two-hundred, or so; mostly of the fraternity and sorority persuasion. Speaking of which, I hear you came with Maxine. Where is she?"

"She's around somewhere. We kind of got separated when we first came in. She went to put your birthday present with the others, and I let her."

"You mean no birthday present from you?" Hayden cracked.

"Yeah, like you need a present from me," Jeffrey returned. "Hell, how do you buy for someone who's got it all anyway?"

Hayden shook his head and smiled. "Ya know, I think you'll make a great politician one day."

"What do you mean?" Jeffrey asked.

"Nothing, forget it. But listen, I do have to go mingle, so make yourself at home, eat and drink to your heart's content, and I'll catch up with you in a little while, alright?"

"Yeah thanks, and listen, happy birthday, Five… really. I'll buy you a beer sometime."

Hayden winked, and then turned and disappeared into the crowd.

Jeffrey proceeded in the opposite direction until he made his way to the other side of the room, where, underneath a grand, almost imposing chandelier, a marble stairway descended from the second floor like the rippling white train of a wedding dress. And that's when he saw her, standing to the side of the rich walnut banister. Stunning, sexy, and all by her lonesome, Jeffrey sauntered toward her, and said, "Excuse me, I don't normally do this, but I have to tell you... you're absolutely the most beautiful thing I've ever seen. My name's Jeffrey Marks. What's yours?"

"I know who you are," She replied, her voice as delicate as her long and silky-fine blonde hair. "You're Maxine's date. She pointed you out earlier. You used to play football for Riley."

"So she's told you about me, eh?"

"Just the things I asked her."

"I see... so what's your name, anyway?"

"Rebecca Graham."

"So you're the one then?"

"The one what?" Rebecca asked, her hypnotic dark eyes basking in the glow of her alluring smile.

"The one engaged to Hayden Riley V, of course."

"Oh that," she said.

"Well it's true, isn't it?"

"I suppose," Rebecca replied indifferently.

"Well aren't you excited about it?" Jeffrey asked, as he ran his fingers through his wavy black hair.

Rebecca scanned the length of Jeffrey's sturdy frame, not once, but twice, before she said, "Let's talk about something else."

"Why?"

"Why not?"

"Okay, what then?"

Rebecca toyed with the ends of her hair, her large diamond engagement ring screaming like a traffic light all the while, and mouthed, "You."

Jeffrey shifted his weight as if to disguise his growing hardness, but as his mind continued to drift between Rebecca's raw sensuality and her plunging neckline, he realized it was of little use. "What about me?" He queried.

"Well, let's see... I could ask you where you're from, but I already know. You're from Avondale. You came here on a football scholarship but didn't like the coach so you quit. Since then you've been working construction. How's that for starters?"

"Not bad."

"I also know that you went out a few times with a girl named Carla Winters."

"How do you know that?"

"A friend of a friend."

"Small world," Jeffrey remarked.

"Not according to her," Rebecca confessed, as her eyes once again climbed the length of Jeffrey's sturdy frame.

"I see," Jeffrey responded after clearing his throat. "And you, where are you from?"

Rebecca smiled. "I'm from Stratford."

Jeffrey returned the smile, and said, "Hell, we played you guys in my sophomore year of high school. Too bad we didn't meet back then."

"You probably had a girlfriend anyway."

"So?" Jeffrey countered.

"So that's pretty daring."

"What's wrong with daring?"

"Nothing. Of course, you know what they say, don't you Mr. Marks?"

"No, what do they say Miss Graham?"

"They say that all good things take time... so maybe it's better this way."

"Yeah, well you know what I say?"

"No, what do you say?"

Jeffrey moved a step closer to Rebecca. "I say there's no time like the present."

"Hmm, I think I might like what you say better," Rebecca suggested, her voice hovering just above a whisper.

Jeffrey cleared his throat again, and said, "I'm getting thirsty. Would you like a drink?"

"That depends."

"On what?"

Rebecca caressed her pearl necklace for a couple of lingering moments, her long and perfectly manicured fingernails grazing the milky-white skin just above her cleavage, before answering, "On whether I'll be drinking alone."

"Not a chance," Jeffrey returned softly. "Although I doubt your fiancé would appreciate it."

"Don't worry about Hayden, he's off playing host."

"I never worry about rich people."

"What do you worry about then?"

"Right now the only thing I'm worried about is how long I have to wait before I find out how daring you are."

Rebecca stared at Jeffrey until little by little... bit by bit... and piece by piece, she felt herself being fondled... embraced... and finally, consumed by the burning desire in his passionate blue eyes, and she murmured, "Not long. Not long at all."

Shelton House, one of three sorority houses located on campus, stood above the banks of the Cedar River, its ivy-covered walls surrounded by towering evergreens that otherwise only sparsely decorated the rambling University landscape. During the day it looked like just another aged building, albeit its recently painted pillars and entryway. During the night, however, it loomed under murky clouds like an ominous shadow, albeit the burning bedroom lamps that gave it life.

Jeffrey waited outside, beyond a cluster of trees, his dark figure lost amid the cool midnight air – warmed only after Rebecca snuck him in through the backdoor, where inside the basement's fiery solitude, her fingers dug into his flesh, her quivering voice whispered his name over and over, and her hips joined his in ardent stride, until what began as an impetuous dare had become an unbridled quest for more – culminating in more lies, more deceit and more risk.

Still, Jeffrey remained largely indifferent to it all, for they were not his lies, it was not his deceit, and the only risk he feared was that of Rebecca giving him the boot before he gave it to her. As such, he was quick to dismiss Rebecca's concerns as nothing more than paranoia. "It's normal," he would say. "You're just feeling a little guilty. That and you're scared of getting caught because it would mean giving up all his money. But don't worry about it, Hayden's too busy bein' rich to ever suspect a thing. Trust me on that, okay? He ain't that smart. Trust me."

And then one night while Rebecca was in the throes of trusting Jeffrey, Hayden and Maxine emerged from the stairwell, where the weak glow of buzzing light bulbs callously shattered Hayden's dreams. "Maxine suspected that something was going on," he began. "I didn't want to believe her, figuring she was just trying to get back at you, Jeffrey, for the way you're always dumping on her. But for weeks on end she's insisted. And now… and now," Hayden mumbled, before the sight of his fiancé tangled up in a way that he, himself, had only imagined, pushed him to tears. Pushing Jeffrey, on the other hand (with no job to return to and no finished basement to sleep in), to take the money he managed to save, and run.

And run he did – to Taylor University, where, after he arrived, the coach changed his mind and decided not to give him a tryout for the upcoming season – to Fuller State, where he was given a hasty tryout, and then promptly told, "Thanks, but no thanks," – to George William College, where he couldn't pass the physical – to Piedmont University, where he failed to show up before the college deadline, let alone take a physical – to Arbor Square, Scottsburg, Salem and Bedford, small cities with limited job opportunities – back to Avondale, where he stayed just long enough to leave his mother a bag full of half-baked excuses and 'borrow' some of her hard earned money for his efforts – then finally, to Muncie, where he held eight different jobs in as many years, before landing work in a sheet metal factory only to break his leg falling off a ladder. Yet, it was during this period when Jeffrey, not only learned to enjoy the leisurely lifestyle that came with collecting unemployment and disability (which he did for the next eighteen months), but also had his first steady girlfriend in longer than he could remember.

Rhea Mills, a part-time community college student, wannabe painter, and the vulnerable young mother of two, stood behind the checkout counter at Muncie Lumber and Hardware (where she also worked thirty-plus hours a week), trying to explain to a customer why a particular brand of tool was not on sale.

"Well it oughta be goddamn-it! What the hell's the difference anyway?"

Rhea stood her ground, her long eyelashes flashing as she smiled at the customer, and said, "The manufacturer, sir. It's not the same manufacturer."

"Oh bullshit on the manufacturer. Get me the goddamn store manager, he'll figure it out. Nothin' worse than havin' to talk man-talk with a girl. Christ Almighty!"

"I'm sorry sir," Rhea responded, her voice as calm and cool as a fresh spring day, "but the manager's not in. And even if he was he'd tell you the same thing I'm tellin' you now. Okay?"

27

"No, it's not okay. In fact, I doubt you even have a clue what he might say. Now get him on the phone."

"I'm sorry sir, I can't do that," Rhea replied.

"Listen you little uppity bitch, I said get him on the phone. And do it before I climb over there and get him on the phone myself."

Jeffrey, who, up until this point, had been mildly entertained by the irascible customer and the cute cashier, finally stepped forward, and snapped, "Hey pal, I don't feel like standing here all day, so either pay for your crap or move on."

"Mind your own fuckin' business," the customer snapped, without turning to look at Jeffrey.

Jeffrey glanced at Rhea (who by now was hoping that somebody, anybody, would intercede), before calmly placing his items on the counter. "Look-it bud, as long as I have to wait for you to throw your little hissy-fit, it is my fuckin' business. Got it?"

"The only thing I got," the customer declared, while keeping his focus solely on Rhea, "is that you're nothin' but a smart-mouth punk."

Although Jeffrey was no longer in football shape, the fact that he added a few soft pounds over the years actually broadened his chest and shoulders to the point where he filled a doorway pretty damn well. Yet, it wasn't until the customer whipped his head sideways and added, "Now keep your mouth shut before I make you shut it," that he saw Jeffrey for the first time.

Jeffrey smiled. "Really, and just how do you see yourself doing that?" He asked, as he folded his healthy arms.

There was no response. The customer simply glared at him for a couple of moments, and then stormed off, leaving his 'must-have' screwdriver sitting on the counter.

Rhea smiled warmly, and said, "Thank-you. We're a little short on help today so I'm not sure what would have happened if you weren't here. My name's Rhea, by the way."

Jeffrey returned the smile. "Rhea what?" He asked.

"Rhea Mills."

"Hi Rhea Mills," Jeffrey said, extending his hand. "My name's Jeffrey Marks."

"Hi Jeffrey," she returned, while embracing his gesture. "It's a pleasure to meet you."

Within a week Rhea and Jeffrey's handshake had turned into handholding. Within two it had become an unavoidable, highly charged sexual encounter, prompted by Rhea's confession that her attraction for Jeffrey had been instant – consummated, in turn, when Jeffrey determined that 'instant' was just another word for 'easy.'

Still, with nothing else on his plate at the time, nothing that didn't require some kind of effort in return, Jeffrey decided that easy was good, easy was comfortable, easy was... well, plain and simple, easy was just flat out easy.

Easy, that is, until a year floated by and Rhea would no longer wait for Jeffrey to close down the bar before dropping in for a late night "special" – easy, that is, until Rhea questioned why she, a single mother of two, took her boyfriend out on more dates than he took her – easy, that is, until she brought up the subject of Jeffrey getting a job – easy, that is, until she voiced her concerns that while Jeffrey enjoyed her kids, he seemed to enjoy them much more from a distance – easy, that is, until she raised the issue of commitment, and solicited his opinions on marriage – easy, that is, until Jeffrey concluded that the sex wasn't worth it and the only thing easy, was, in fact, taking the easy way out.

So he did, when, without so much as a goodbye to Rhea, he got up one morning and decided to leave Indiana altogether. Travel the world! Sail the seven seas! Explore the grand ol' USA! Or, in the alternative, at least move somewhere else. But where, he wondered? West Virginia, where his mother was getting ready to move – Florida, where the warm weather would be good for his leg, even though it had long healed – Kentucky, home to red clay, bluegrass, and mint juleps – or, someplace out west, perhaps? Someplace his worn-down pickup truck could still get to without dying along the way. Someplace fresh, someplace pretty, someplace, say, like Colorado... where the sky is blue, the land never-ending, and everyday is one more day farther removed from his nondescript past.

Colorado Springs shimmered beneath the horizon like the timeless jewels on a king's crown. Strong, but precious, brilliant, yet refined, its grandeur was surpassed only by the splendor of the mountains that stood guard over her.

As Jeffrey soon discovered after his unemployment checks ran out and he wound up taking a job pouring drinks in the Stink Water

Saloon, Colorado Springs also had its share of beer-chugging, backslapping, suburban-loving mountain men. More importantly, however, it was a town with great lookin' ladies... lots and lots and lots of 'em. Single, married, no matter, Jeffrey's new job gave him an opportunity to mingle with 'em all. They'd ask for a drink, and he'd pour two – he'd hope for a tip, and pocket phone numbers in the process. It wasn't long, in fact, before Jeffrey was friendly with more people than at anytime since high school.

It also wasn't long before Jeffrey became known around town as, 'The Fastest Drink in the West,' a distinction that earned him more money than he ever thought possible. Enough money to rent a furnished one-bedroom apartment – enough money to send his mother a plane ticket should she decide to come out for a visit – enough money to buy a stereo, TV, clothes, and even a used, but well maintained pickup truck.

It was not, however, enough money to keep up with a cocaine habit, a habit which began when the owner of Stink Water's, Big Matt McDuff, called him into his office after the bar closed one night, and said, "I gotta little present for ya... help you celebrate your two-year anniversary."

Jeffrey glanced at his boss, a wide man with hard eyes, leathery skin and the kind of soft, friendly smile that seemed out of place with the rest of his features, particularly his gravelly voice, and asked, "Has it been that long, Duffy?"

"Yep, it has. And just so ya know, I'm real happy with the work you do too," Duffy said, his ponytail dancing to the rhythm of his bobbing head. "Thinkin' of making you the manager. Think you could handle the job?"

"You're kidding, right?"

"Hey," Duffy, countered, "don't look so surprised."

"I just never figured... you know," Jeffrey suggested, shrugging his shoulders.

Duffy lumbered to the other side of his cluttered desk and sat down. "Yeah, well," he said, as the chair moaned while he adjusted his weight, "I've been thinkin' about it for a couple months now."

"I don't know what to say?" Jeffrey responded, as he slumped into a chair opposite his boss.

30

Duffy smiled, his eyes all but disappearing as they slipped deep inside their sockets, and asked, "So you think you can handle it, or what?"

Jeffrey stretched out his legs, cupped his hands behind his head, and exhaled, "Sure, why not?"

"Well for starters, not everyone wants the added hours or the added responsibility. And since I know you like your time off, I just thought the job may be more than you're willing to bite off. It will, however, come with a pretty good pay raise."

"Really now, like what?" Jeffrey returned, his voice jumping with interest.

Duffy dipped his head from side to side. "I'm not sure yet. Some of it'll be in the form of money, some in incentives. I just gotta sit down and put pen to paper. Wanted to see if you were interested first."

Jeffrey let his arms fall over the sides of the chair, before replying, "I dunno Duff, it sounds pretty tempting."

"Good," Duffy said, as he rested his thick forearms on the desk. "I was hoping you'd think so. But listen, we're not gonna make the move for another few months... until after the first of the year. So if you wanna roll it around till then, feel free."

"Whatever you say, Duffy... whatever you say."

Duffy twisted around in his chair and slid open the door to his credenza. "I say it's time for a toast."

"What, you want me to get a couple of beers, or somethin'?" Jeffrey asked.

"Fuck the beer, you ever do blow?" Duffy countered, as he twisted back with a mirror in hand.

"Been around it, never done it," Jeffrey said, shaking his head.

Duffy pulled a vial from his shirt pocket and proceeded to unload the white powder in the middle of the mirror. It wasn't until he formed a myriad of lines the length of a tall man's index finger, however, that he finally said, "Yeah, well, just remember, you gotta pair of virgin nostrils there, so you may feel a bit of a sting. Before ya know it though, it'll disappear and you'll be wantin' more... lots n' lots more."

"Yeah?" Jeffrey asked eagerly.

"Oh yeah," Duffy asserted, his face lighting up with excitement. "This shit is one great buzz. Now get a dollar out of your pocket, roll *it up nice n' tight... but not too tight 'cuz ya don't want any problems suckin' the shit through it, and help yourself."*

And help himself, Jeffrey did – to every line, every gram, every ounce and every eight-ball he could get his hands on. No matter when, no matter where, no matter how much the cost, Jeffrey was ready, willing, and able – until what had originally ignited in the belly of curiosity evolved into a love so deep, for an addiction so consuming, night often swallowed day, day often regurgitated fits of restless sleep, and Jeffrey was mindlessly content to survive solely on the frenzied energy that for the next year, stewed between.

Any opportunity to manage the Stink Water Saloon was – poof – gone! In fact, the only reason Jeffrey managed to keep his bartending job was because Big Matt McDuff felt responsible for having fed him cocaine in the first place. Jeffrey, however, was hardly concerned with the reason, only that it provided him cash – his gateway to the White Lady, Snow Goddess, and Mother of Pearl. Still, Duffy's guilt did not run so deep that it included keeping a blind eye to a pair of sticky fingers. Therefore, when he caught Jeffrey dipping into the register after the bar closed one night, he stormed up behind him, snatched the money from his quivering hand, and snapped, "How much you rippin' me for Jeffrey? How much ya got here?"

"What? What? I, I, didn't... I, I..."

Duffy rifled through the money then abruptly shook his head. "Fifty bucks," he said incredulously. "You're stealin' fifty bucks. How long you been doin' this, huh? How long?"

"Duff, I didn't... I, I didn't..."

"Shut up Jeffrey!" Duffy growled. "Just shut up and listen. You're a fuckin' mess, okay? An absolute fuckin' mess. You're sweatin', ya stink, ya can't put a thought together to save your life, and now you're stealin'. And it's all because of a stupid little drug that you let get way out of hand. Well I got news for you partner, you need to take a look at yourself... and I mean quick-like. You got me?"

Jeffrey lowered his head in silence.

"I tried to be your friend," Duffy continued, his tone soiled with anger and disappointment. "I tried to be your friend, and this is how you repay me."

Jeffrey swallowed hard but otherwise remained silent.

"Well here's more news for ya, pal... there's nothin' left for me to do now but throw your ass out of here."

Jeffrey shuffled his feet before lifting his head, his dilated pupils dancing nervously as they scanned Duffy's pained expression. "You can't," he implored, his one-time cavalier attitude now just a shadow of itself. "You can't."

"Yeah, well, I am Jeffrey, and it's nobody's fault but yours. Nobody."

"Please Duff, ya gotta... ya gotta help me. You gotta help me. Okay... okay?"

"Tell me why...why should I help you after what you did to me?"

"B'cuz I got...I got nothin'. All my st'...stuff...I hocked it. And my landlord, Duff...I'm gonna...I'm gonna lose...I got n'...nowhere...I got nothin'," Jeffrey stammered, as tears filled his eyes.

"Should've thought of that before, Jeffrey."

"Please Duff... please."

"I dunno Jeffrey. I just don't know."

"Duff," Jeffrey pleaded, "you're my last... you're my only... my only hope."

Duffy shook his head for several moments before reaching into his pocket, slowly... begrudgingly. "Here, take this," he said, his words marked by a languishing sigh as he stuffed two hundred bucks into Jeffrey's waiting palm. "It's all I can do for ya. But you do yourself a favor. Get a shower, get a meal, and get cleaned up. And until you do, I don't wanna see you back here again. Got it?"

Jeffrey got it, alright – two grams of coke, to be exact. He also got some personal items from his apartment then hopped into his pickup truck, where, hand in hand, he and his favorite white lady rode off into the darkness.

"Daddy, come on out here, I think you're gonna wanna see this," Frankie called to her father just as she finished tying her hair into a ponytail.

"What Frankie? I'm just about to head out to the stables. Told Danny and Mike I'd be there by seven."

"You're gonna be late then," Frankie responded, as the screen door slammed behind her.

"Frankie..."

"C'mon, Daddy, hurry up. The door'll survive."

"I'm comin', I'm comin'," Sam Cochran muttered as he hustled his way through the tidy ranch house and joined his only child on the front porch.

"Looks like someone crashed," Frankie said.

"I'll say," Sam replied, as he panned the length of the wood fence that stood between his property and the dirt road some two hundred yards away. *"Looks like they tore down the whole westerly section."*

"It's just a fence," Frankie reminded her father before jumping off the porch, her young, athletic legs holding a steady pace as she traversed the scraggly patches of grass on her way to the accident.

"Yeah, but I just painted it," Sam muttered, as he bound down the steps and gave chase, his forty-five-year-old-legs absorbing only a fraction of the shock they used to.

A few minutes later Frankie was eyeballing the damaged pickup truck. *"Looks bad,"* she commented when her winded father finally approached.

"Anybody hurt?"

"I dunno," Frankie replied, as she peered through the cracked windshield, the early morning sunlight throwing back a near perfect reflection of her blossoming splendor. *"There's no one inside."*

Sam dragged the back of his hand across the sweat on his forehead. *"Man, I can't believe anybody could've got out of this thing, much less go for help."*

"Well if they went for help," Frankie said, as she walked around to the back of the truck, her emerald green eyes wincing at the sight of the damage, *"you'd think they would've come to our house, wouldn't you?"*

Sam nodded. *"Yes, I would, honey. Then again, they might not have been thinking all that clearly."*

"Maybe they tried to and didn't make it."

"You think maybe they're someplace back the other way?" Sam queried, as he lowered himself to one knee.

"Unless you're about to tell me they're underneath the truck," Frankie cracked, as she pulled up next to her father.

"No, nobody there," Sam hastily concluded, before straightening up. *"Let's look around though. Maybe they got thrown, or, like you say darlin', maybe they tried to make it up to the house, in which case we might have a little searchin' ahead of us."*

Frankie gazed at her father, a man whose affable demeanor often belied his unflinching resolve, and asked, "You want me to go n' call the stables first? Tell Danny and Mike you might not be there for awhile?"

"No, first things first. You go that way," Sam said, pointing north, "and I'll look around here some more. Okay?"

"Okay," Frankie replied, but just as she turned to head off, she turned back. "Daddy?"

"Yeah Frankie, what is it?"

"You don't think they're dead, do you? I mean, I really don't want to find a dead body."

Sam sighed, before responding, "I don't want you to either honey," his gentle tone masking the exploding image of his beautiful wife collapsing in front of his then five-year-old daughter. "I don't want you to either."

Frankie smiled warmly. "I love you Sam."

"Thank you, honey. I love you too. Now let's get on with it... alright?"

Frankie nodded, and then turned away from her father once again.

Sam wiped a bit of dust from his eyes (the same bit of dust that gathered whenever his daughter said she loved him), and headed for the drainage ditch across the road. It was there that he soon found Jeffrey. "Frankie," he yelled, "before dropping his ear to Jeffrey's chest. "At least he's breathin'," Sam mumbled as his head sprang up and he called for his daughter once more.

"Daddy? Daddy?" Frankie called back, her voice bouncing through the still morning air as she ran.

"Over here," Sam directed. "I'm over here."

"Daddy?"

"In the drainage ditch, honey."

"What'd you find?" Frankie panted, as her hiking boots skidded across the dirt road then down the embankment of the ditch. "What'd you find?"

"He's alive, but he's unconscious," Sam replied hastily.

"Looks like he was bleeding too," Frankie added, as she surveyed the trail of dried red stretching from Jeffrey's nose to his Adam's apple.

"You need to call Doc Morris, honey. Tell him there's been an accident at our place. Tell him it's an emergency."

"You think we oughta call an ambulance instead?"

"No time. The hospital's sixty... seventy miles from here. Doc Morris is only ten minutes. Bring back the flatbed too. We'll take him back to the house in that."

Doc Morris, a bald-headed, bespectacled man with a short white beard and a gentle touch, carefully situated his stethoscope between the abrasions on Jeffrey's chest. But just as he closed in for a listen Jeffrey's eyes fluttered open and he asked, "Who the hell are you?"

"Well now, I've been expecting you to wake up," Doc Morris said calmly, though Jeffrey's sudden awakening had indeed startled him. "I'm Dr. Morris, but you can call me Doc. Most everyone does."

"Where the hell am I?" Jeffrey asked as he fidgeted to get a better view of his unfamiliar surroundings.

"Easy son, easy," Doc Morris said, easing Jeffrey back to the feathery pillows supporting his head. "You've had an accident, and though you appear to be fine, you have a variety of cuts and bruises that may give you a little discomfort."

Jeffrey licked the chapped dryness of his lips, and then swallowed, although his throat was parched as well.

"Here, drink this," Doc Morris instructed as he reached for the glass of water beside the bed.

Jeffrey propped himself up on his elbows while Doc Morris fed him a straw.

"How's that, better?"

Jeffrey nodded until Doc Morris pulled the straw away, at which point he once again asked, "Where the hell am I?"

"You're in Brisbane, Colorado – the home of Sam and Frankie Cochran, to be exact. They found you a couple of hours ago. You were lying in the drainage ditch across from their property."

"My truck... what about my truck?"

Doc Morris shook his head. "Sorry son, I don't think it's gonna make it. Tow truck's on the way now. But just in case, Henry, from over at Henry's Garage, said he'd hang onto it for ya until you decide."

"What's to decide? I don't have any money to fix it even if I want to."

"Well that's not important anyhow. What's important is that you managed to survive."

"Speaking of survival," Jeffrey said, his finger nervously tapping the mattress, "did they find anything inside?"

"A suitcase full of clothes. The suitcase is a little banged up, but the clothes are okay."

"That it?" Jeffrey asked, (tap, tap, tap, tap, tap).

"Why, was there something more?" Doc Morris asked curiously. "I mean if you think there is we can always have Henry go through the truck once he gets it back to the garage."

Jeffrey quickly replayed the events leading up to the accident, remembered that he pitched each beer bottle out the window after he drank it and the empty vial of cocaine only moments before he saw the deer, and said, "No, come to think of it there isn't," (tap, tap, tap, tap, tap).

"Good, then we got all your stuff out for ya," Doc Morris concluded.

Jeffrey nervously scanned the room, the anxious burn of coke residue smoldering inside him like smoke from screeching brakes. "What the hell happened anyway?" (Tap, tap, tap, tap, tap).

Doc Morris shook his head. "We were hoping you could tell us."

"Listen, is it okay if I sit all the way up?" (Tap, tap, tap, tap, tap).

"I don't know, do you feel like you can?"

"I think so, yeah," Jeffrey replied.

"Okay, let's give it a try then. Slowly...slowly...that's it son...nice n' easy...nice n' easy," Doc Morris instructed while repositioning the pillows as Jeffrey winced himself into a sitting position. "Better?"

"Much. Thanks," Jeffrey replied, keeping his hands buried underneath the blanket to hide his tap, tap, tap, tap, tapping.

"Don't thank me, thank the Cochran's."

"Where are they anyway?"

"Right around the corner. Sam... Frankie, come on in," Doc Morris called out. "The boy's up and around."

Sam Cochran, a well built man with even features and smooth skin (notwithstanding a weathered glow, courtesy of too often sleeping under the stars without a tent), put out his hand, then immediately thought better of it and held it up instead. "Hi son, name's Sam Cochran. How you feeling?"

Jeffrey nodded. "All things considered I guess I'm okay," (tap, tap, tap, tap, tap). "Thanks for asking," (tap, tap, tap, tap, tap).

"And this is my daughter, Frankie," Sam said, stepping off to the side.

"Hi," Frankie said, her wholesome smile blending perfectly with the soft yellows and starch whites of the bedroom.

Jeffrey returned the smile, and replied, "Hi, my name's Jeffrey," (tap, tap, tap, tap, tap). "Jeffrey Marks. And listen, I'm real sorry if I caused damage to anything," (tap, tap, tap, tap, tap).

"You don't remember?" Sam asked.

"The last thing I remember," Jeffrey began, fighting the urge to focus solely on Frankie's good looks, "is that I hit a deer," (tap, tap, tap, tap, tap). "At least I think it was a deer. After that I woke up here. Was there... was there more?" (Tap, tap, tap, tap, tap).

Frankie scrunched up her perfectly shaped nose. "A little fence trauma," she said before her father had a chance to answer. "Nothing that can't be repaired."

"So what were you doin' out this way, anyway?" Sam asked, all the while thinking to himself, 'a little fence trauma, my ass.'

"Just driving. No place special in mind."

"Where you from?"

Jeffrey turned to face Doc Morris. "Colorado Springs," (tap, tap, tap, tap, tap). "Lost my job and was... I dunno, I guess I was feeling sorry for myself, so I got in my truck and," (tap, tap, tap, tap, tap), "you know, just sort of took off," (tap, tap, tap, tap, tap). "Wasn't thinking about where I was going – I guess because I've got no where to go to," (tap, tap, tap, tap, tap).

"Do you have any family son?" Sam queried, his eyes narrowing in a look of concern.

Jeffrey nodded. "A mother in West Virginia," (tap, tap, tap, tap, tap). "I talked to her a week or two ago so she doesn't know I lost my job yet. And as long as I'm okay," (tap, tap, tap, tap, tap), "I just as soon not tell her about my accident. She'll just worry," (tap, tap, tap, tap, tap).

"Well listen," Sam said, approaching the bed, "Doc told us that you don't need a hospital or anything, just a week or two of rest. Maybe longer. Either way, with that truck of yours out of commission, and no place else to go... well, I just don't think I'd be a very good

Christian if I didn't open up my house to ya. So stay as long as necessary, alright?"

"Hey, that's awfully kind of you," Jeffrey feigned with an 'aw-shucks' authenticity. "But I couldn't impose," (tap, tap, tap, tap, tap). "I really couldn't," (tap, tap, tap, tap, tap).

"Don't be silly, Frankie n' I both realize that having a stranger around may be a bit uncomfortable. But in all honesty, that's the way we do things around here. Besides, if you're looking for work... well then, there's plenty of it right here on our ranch. We've got a bunk house with all the comforts of home right next to the stables. Anyway, you get better and then if you want, we'll sit down and talk about it. How's that sound?"

"I dunno," Jeffrey said, twisting his head sideways. "It sounds like I crashed into the right place," (tap, tap, tap, tap, tap).

The Cochran Ranch, though nestled between a vast array of towering cliffs and snowcapped mountains was neither particularly large, nor particularly profitable. It was, however, home to some of the hardest working people Jeffrey had ever been around. And though he carried the conspicuous distinction of having never been on a horse, much less worked on a ranch, with a new attitude – one fueled by the nourishment of a fresh start under the fresh skies of a ruggedly beautiful land, and a willingness to learn – an effort buoyed by the camaraderie and support of those he worked alongside (including Frankie, who regularly schooled him on the finer points of riding), in a year's time Jeffrey more than held his own.

Thereafter, it wasn't long before Jeffrey was accompanying Sam and Frankie to the weekly horse auctions in Brisbane; a situation that began when Sam realized that Jeffrey had, what he termed, 'an instinctive eye for a good hoof'; a situation that continued because Frankie wanted his company.

"I like him... a lot," she told her father over coffee one morning, though the subtle hesitation in her voice suggested something more.

"A lot... as in you like him a lot?" Sam asked, his own voice growing pensive. "Or you think that maybe you...?"

Frankie bit her bottom lip and nodded.

"I see. And how does Jeffrey feel?"

"I haven't told him yet. At least not that part of it."

"Hmm," Sam poured out with a sigh.

Frankie swallowed. "You don't like him, do you?"

Sam nodded. "Actually I do, Frankie. I'm just not sure we know enough about him yet."

"Why do you say that, daddy? I mean he's been working here for almost a year-and-a-half and I feel like I know plenty about him."

"You do... like what?"

"Like, he lost his job in Colorado Springs because the bar closed up – like he was engaged to be married but once he lost his job, he lost his fiancé – like he's an only child whose father walked out on him when he was two-years-old – like he sends money home to his mother whenever he can afford to – like he broke his leg in college and had to forfeit his football scholarship – like...

"Honey, honey," Sam interjected, as he cupped his hand over his daughter's. "Those are things about his past. They're events, and yes, they are important... every last one of them. But what about now? What qualities do you know today?"

After a moment of quiet reflection Frankie pulled her eyes from the table and looked at her father. "Do you remember what you once told me about horses?"

Sam shrugged. "Probably, but I'm not sure what you're getting at."

Frankie smiled. "You once told me that when horses come in contact with somebody they can sense the true nature of that person. Like a dog can spot fear, a horse can spot kindness, you said."

"Honey, that doesn't mean..."

"Hang on daddy, I'm not saying that I know Jeffrey because of the way our horses respond to him. I'm simply saying that over the last... well, however long it's been, I've come to know Jeffrey as nothing but extremely kind and caring. On top of that he's been a perfect gentleman towards me. The horses, they just respond accordingly. Does that... does that make sense?"

"Listen Frankie, no matter what I say you're gonna spend time with Jeffrey and that's fine. Really, it is," Sam replied, as he squeezed his daughter's hand. "I just don't want to see you get hurt, that's all. And I'm not saying Jeffrey's a bad guy and he's gonna hurt you. I'm just saying it takes a long time before you know the inside of a person... not past events in his life, but the actual person."

"I understand daddy. I just hope you understand where I'm coming from too."

"*I do, Frankie, don't worry.*"

"*Then why do you look so troubled, father of mine?*"

Sam shrugged. "*I'm not really troubled. A little concerned, maybe... not troubled.*"

"*About what?*"

"*Nothin', forget it.*"

"*Forget nothin', tell me.*"

"*Fine, just don't get mad, okay?*"

"*Sam...*"

"*Okay, fine, I'm a little concerned about the age difference between...*"

"*Whoa, whoa, whoa, don't you dare bring up age,*" *Frankie playfully warned.*

"*Well?*"

"*Well nothin' daddy – aren't you the one always telling everybody that I was a grown woman the day I was born?*"

"*But you're still only twenty-two,*" *Sam countered.*

"*Yes, only twenty-two, but when I decided to work the ranch rather than go off to college, who's the one who said I was probably too mature for college kids anyway?*"

Sam frowned. "*Did I say that?*"

"*Sam...*"

"*Okay, fine, I said it.*"

"*And besides,*" *Frankie added,* "*he's not that much older than I am.*"

"*Twelve years,*" *Sam remarked.*

"*Oh, okay, so should I not like him because an entire decade stands between us? I like you and more than two decades separate us,*" *Frankie quipped.*

"*Thanks, kiddo, I like you too. That's why I get concerned.*"

"*I know,*" *Frankie responded, as she slipped her hand out from underneath her father's.* "*And I'll be careful.*"

Yet, as the days embraced the weeks and the weeks embraced the months, Frankie's caution embraced Jeffrey's passion, and his careless seed of life.

"*But don't worry, we're gonna get married,*" *Jeffrey explained when confronted by Sam.*

"*Yeah – when?*"

41

"Obviously before Frankie has the baby."

"But she's not due for another six months – which means you're getting married sometime between tomorrow and the next five and-a-half months. So which is it?"

"Actually I suggested to Frankie that we get married in another three months – May 10th to be exact. The same day you n' your wife were married."

And Sam was content. And Sam was pleased. Sam even gave Jeffrey a new pickup truck as a token of his happiness.

But Jeffrey was not content – not since his conquest of Frankie had grown stale. Jeffrey was not pleased – not with Frankie's burgeoning belly, the thought of stretch marks, or having to be responsible for a family he never wanted in the first place. As such, on the morning of their wedding day, Jeffrey was also long-gone – leaving Colorado as fast and as furiously as his ticket to freedom, his new pickup truck, would carry him.

And in the three-plus years that followed his exit, Jeffrey bounced from town to town, job to job, bar to bar, and woman to woman, before bouncing all the way back to his mother's house in Port Charles, West Virginia.

"You know what I think, Jeffrey?" Flora Marks asked her son after hearing the unfortunate details of his unsuccessful job hunting stint in Clarksville.

Jeffrey lifted his hanging head, waited for his mother's cigarette smoke to float by, and replied, "No, what do you think? And just so you know, I don't want to hear you say, 'you've just had a long run of bad luck, son.' I know my lucks been bad ma. I'm tired of knowin' my luck's been bad. I've been everywhere between here and Colorado and that's all I ever got was more bad luck. For once, I need something good to happen. Fuck, ma, I deserve somethin' good for a change."

"That's not what I was going to say anyway, Jeffrey."

"What then?"

Flora Marks stabbed her cigarette in the ashtray before pushing the smoldering mess off to the side. "I was gonna say that I think you should go to this high school reunion of yours."

"Yeah, why is that?" Jeffrey asked, his eyebrows threatening to make direct contact.

"Well son," Flora began, "I just figured since you weren't havin' much luck with your present life, you might want to revisit your past."

"What's that gonna do?"

"I'm not really sure," Flora replied, her puffy cheeks jiggling as she shook her head. "But I've heard it said that a person's past is the door to their future. So maybe it's not too late, Jeffrey. Maybe this little trip down memory lane will help you figure out what went wrong, allowing you, in turn, to start over. New slate, new prospects, that sort of thing. Besides," Flora added, her eyes lighting up about as much as a pair of weary red eyes could, "I hear your old girlfriend Jennie is gonna be there. I hear she's looking forward to seeing you; very much so."

"Yeah... where'd you hear that?"

"Same place I heard that she never really got over you."

"Oh yeah?" Jeffrey remarked, his eyebrows twisting off in different directions.

"I also heard that she divorced extremely well. Evidently she married some bigwig doctor, but when she couldn't have kids he sent her packing... with a bundle of money, I might add."

"Ma, are you gonna tell me where you got your information, or not?"

"Billy Johnson's mother."

"Billy Johnson... my Billy Johnson?"

"Uh-huh."

"So that's how they knew where to send the invitation. Hell and I didn't even know you still talked to his mother."

"Hey listen son, just 'cuz you stopped talking to your old friends doesn't mean I have to."

"Yeah, yeah, yeah," Jeffrey sneered. "It's my fault they stopped callin'."

Flora pulled her purse across the kitchen table and dug her hand inside for a fresh pack of cigarettes. "I didn't say it was your fault. So let's not have that conversation again, okay? Let's talk about this reunion of yours instead. It's in one week," she said, while peeling off the cellophane. "Now the way I see it, you can go buy yourself a nice new suit, drive that truck of yours back to Avondale, shouldn't take but a day's ride, find yourself a hotel room and see what it's all about – especially since that old girlfriend of yours is wanting to see you.

Who knows, maybe the ol' sparks will fly again. Shouldn't be too difficult – not if she's got all that money to go along with that pretty face I remember her having."

Jeffrey folded his arms and leaned as far back as the vinyl chair would allow. "I dunno ma, I think you might be on to something," he mused. "There's just one problem... actually two problems. I don't have money for a new suit, or a hotel room, which I might actually need for a couple of nights."

"You probably don't have enough spendin' money either," Flora remarked, as her unlit cigarette danced between her lips. "But I was plannin' to cover that too. So now you got no problems... just a decision to make."

"Oh it's made, ma... I'm going. I am absolutely going."

Colonial Banquet Hall was only two miles from Avondale High School, and though Jeffrey was already ten minutes late to the reunion, he sat in his truck scanning the football field – the weathered bleachers and splintered benches – the rusted goal posts, and the drab, off-season grass – each one staring at him with the colorless eyes of a dead man. Yet, Jeffrey stared right back – back to the boisterous crowds of Friday night, back to the glaring lights that shadowed his strides into the end-zone, back to the waiting arms of his cheering teammates and fans, and, of course, back to Jennie.

It wasn't until the 8:20 train screamed its pending arrival at the nearby train station, in fact, that Jeffrey shook off the dust from his past, and muttered, "Who'd believe it? Twenty years and this place still looks like the same ol' shit-hole it used to. Still, you had the time of your life here, Marks – don't forget that. Had your greatest glories, too."

It was another few minutes before Jeffrey broke his own silence again, this time as he pulled his truck into the banquet hall parking lot, and said, "Who knows, maybe the old lady's right. Maybe sparks between me n' Jennie will fire right up. Maybe I'll actually hit the jackpot this time."

Yet, upon entering the party, where he was immediately swallowed up in a pool of hugs and high-fives, Jeffrey spotted Jennie halfway across the room. She was standing with a group of people he didn't recognize, looking straight at him and smiling, her face as beautiful as the day he last saw her. When she turned to excuse

44

herself from her conversation, however, Jeffrey also noticed that she had put on some weight – twenty-five, thirty… hell, maybe even forty pounds.

"Holy shit," Jeffrey muttered as he seized Billy Johnson's arm.

"What's up, bud?" Billy asked.

"You're not gonna believe it. You're not gonna fuckin' believe it."

"Believe what?"

"My luck, it just never fuckin' changes."

"Luck… what the hell you talkin' about Jeffrey? What kind of luck?"

"Listen, Billy… remember how I always said I hate fat chicks?"

Billy chuckled. "Yeah, I remember."

"Well… I still do," Jeffrey declared, before he turned… and ran… once again.

The Profundity of Madness

My name is Hubbell Webster... although I've been known to answer to Hub or Dr. Web. This, of course, depends on the mouth calling and the situation beckoning, but for the most part either one will get my attention. Keeping my attention, now that's another story altogether. It seems I've been blessed with a high aptitude; high enough to graduate first in my class at Cambridge Medical School, only to go on and become a psychiatrist, or, as my esteemed colleagues are so fond of saying to anyone mindless enough to pay attention to them, a generously gifted, albeit strange psychiatrist.

Strange psychiatrist? An intriguing play on words, wouldn't you agree? In fact, it might just give new meaning to the term, symmetry – synonymously speaking, of course.

Granted, I have a fondness for sarcasm. And perhaps I'm a bit strange as well. However, it's not as though I'm an abstract painting in a watercolor world. If anything I'm just a lead-pencil doodle who tends to get bored easily.

Let's face it, how many schizophrenics and manic-depressives can you talk to? Indeed, many people find that sort of thing interesting and I guess for a time I did as well. But my god! There are only so many black holes you can dive into before they all start to look the same. Black. Certainly, to condense every one of my patient's problems into the same hermetically sealed jar of psychobabble is wrong. But like I said, I tend to get bored easily.

Besides, why spend time trying to decipher the inner workings of... shall we say... the clinically erratic, when the attendant insurance company is merely going to excrete a mind-numbing, thought provoking, "Hmmmm," before prescribing a hocus-pocus doctor with a pocketful of cheese-whiz pills?

Yes, well, oddly enough that ghastly approach to treatment has worked wonders for those restless, rambunctious and recalcitrant souls looking to spend a bit more time on autopilot. But it does little more than alter the toxicity levels of those looking to ascend from the hellish depths of true madness. That aside, however, why should I be above the, *take two of these every four hours for the rest of your life,* approach to medicine, when to do so is to give up afternoon tee-times with drug reps and insurance company execs?

Truth is, since I've never understood the obsession with chasing little white dimpled balls around a sculpted cow patch, the question is hypothetical at best. Nevertheless, I have played golf. Once. I made it all the way to the sixth hole, a par three I believe it was, only to discover that the game would be far more interesting if played in the image of polo. So – I saddled up my golf cart, grabbed my putter-shaped-mallet and away I went. Unfortunately my enthusiasm for implementing such a unique approach to the game was not shared by others and I was promptly asked to remove myself from the premises. Forever.

Of course, it's not the first time my conduct has dismayed the innocent. In fact, I've been in a situation or two... okay, maybe a situation or fifty, when my behavior has been probed, prodded, and even disemboweled, when I was hardly aware that I had even stepped on the taintless toe of another, let alone disrupted their *snug like a bug in a rug little world*. But you see? One need only be labeled for such perceived misdeeds before the perception becomes the truth. And, upon that inevitable occurrence the veracity, though forever contaminated by whimsical storytelling and self-serving exaggeration, is absolute.

Take that particular summer evening when I was invited to speak at a black-tie affair on the deviant element in society. Since I've always been of the learned opinion that no educated society can actually exist without deviants (for are they not the very reason we pass laws, without which, every last one of us might well fall prey to such behavior?), I found the subject matter rather blasé. Yet, when asked by a well dressed gentleman in the front row if I believed most deviant behavior was confined to the *have-nots* of the world, and after responding, ever so politely, I might add, "Only if stupidity is confined to the *haves*," I felt quite the opposite, as an inspiring sense of amusement pulled hard at my sleeve – culminating in a sudden and rousing desire to moon the audience; surmising, as my ample derriere smiled at the face of the crowd, that such action would be viewed as deviant behavior confined to a prodigiously stupid, but fairly well-to-do *have*. Unfortunately I was not able to discern if the audience found any cracks in the theory of my presentation because I was unceremoniously whisked off the stage.

Yet, like most good tales, this lovely little adventure did not begin to evolve until such time as it began to degenerate. Specifically, by week's end there were widespread stories that before I was so brusquely escorted away, I doused the audience with the primal rumblings of some well-placed flatulence. False to be sure, but, when coupled with a handful of other purported misdeeds, a good ol' fashioned perception was created – one that has since trailed me like a foul odor.

Of course, it all goes back to the premise that I get bored easily; an excuse, that given its puerile implications, is often perceived as short on substance. Nevertheless, it is the truth. How else, in fact, could I possibly explain, with head held high, mind you, the circumstances surrounding the first of my three arrests?

It was a splendid spring day. I, however, was stuck inside the university teaching one of my four weekly classes. I had one eye on a window, where outside I bore witness to the frolic of campus life, and one eye on a student who decided to ask me if the inalienable rights of man call for self-rule, what is it about man's psyche that compels him to exercise his dominion over all other living creatures?

In as much as the question was not only a formidable consequence of absurdity, but a wayward departure from what had been the subject matter as well, I felt no obligation to articulate an answer, be it a sagaciously crafted, long winded soliloquy or a judicious recitation of the obvious.

Nevertheless, when I gazed out the window again, and much to my delight saw a campus security guard lumber inside a neighboring building (while his trusted horse remained tied to a tree), it was the very obvious I could no longer ignore. As a result, I turned to my intellectually challenged student, and asked, "Mr. Beezer, why do the dean and his merry band of regents employ the use of horses to help overweight security guards patrol a small, peaceful school like ours?"

Rather than wait for what likely would have been an inane response, I let the question linger, while I, in turn, made haste for the outdoors, where I freed the animal and climbed aboard. Yet, before embarking on a ride into the great unknown, I directed the glorious creature over to the flowerbeds beneath my second-story classroom, scanned the puzzled faces of the students looking at me through open windows, and proudly declared, "Because they can, Mr. Beezer! Just like I can!"

As for the ride itself? Well, now, let me assure you it was a most splendid experience, for it took me back to the summers of my youth, which, unfortunately ended when I turned sixteen – the year I began my freshman stay at college. (You'll recall that I was blessed, or, cursed as the case may be, with more than my fair share of aptitude). Nevertheless, I had the grand fortune of spending many a wonderful summer on my grandfather's farm, just outside of Chesterfield, New England.

My mother and father, decent souls though they were, often bemoaned, what they called, "Their inability to make contact with me." They found my energy level exacerbating, my interest in discussing politics at the ripe young age of ten, mysteriously curious, and my social skills a cross between Blackbeard The Pirate and Cyrano de Bergerac. Yet, those were some of the very same qualities that reaped my grandfather's attention. "The lad just needs some elbow room, that's all," he would tell my mother. "Give him some space to find himself, and find himself he will."

Unfortunately, I don't think my grandfather ever realized that in my case, finding myself was oft times the beginning to losing myself again, for I have been nothing in my life if not the mouth and morsel of my own food chain.

Nevertheless, my days on the farm were quite memorable. I would awaken each morning at the crack of dawn, throw myself at whatever hearty chore beckoned, although I must admit, milking cows never grabbed me near as much as it most certainly grabbed the cows, and then spend the rest of the day either working or exploring the wilds of the twenty-five hundred acres my grandfather spent a lifetime accumulating. Evenings, on the other hand, were tranquil by comparison, as the sweat of summer fun and toil was replaced by tall tales and wistful moments alongside the crackling flames of majestic bonfires.

Peculiar though it may sound, it was during this time when I began to understand the struggle of life outside of the books I had read; be it an animal fighting to stave off predatory savagery, a crop suffocating via the inclement hands of nature, a farmhand breaking his back to feed a wife and child, or, my grandfather growing older, yet constantly finding the strength to endure the tremendous responsibility he felt for the continued survival of them all.

49

It was also during this time when I first realized that my grandfather possessed a fondness for me like no one before, and I dare say, no one since. Interestingly enough, I did not reach this conclusion because I was showered with unnecessary affection or infused with unworthy praise, measures, that in the seasons of a boy's life I consider marginally beneficial, at best. My reasoning boils down to the simple premise that my grandfather made every conceivable effort to accept and understand that which my parents so freely dismissed as, *my unorthodox composition*, an undertaking, perhaps, without boundary, an objective, heartfelt, yet arguably futile.

Suffice it to say it was a very sad day when my grandfather died. Although strangely enough, I experienced a greater sense of loss when my mother and father sold his property, for on that long, dreary afternoon it was as if my grandfather's spirit was vaporized right before my very eyes. From then on, all communication with my parents was necessity driven. I was in the midst of college life and they... they were in the midst of plowing through my grandfather's hard earned money. Fortunately, grandfather made it impossible for them to squander it all, as I was left with one-half of his estate, money I've since used to repurchase various parcels of his once proud and seductive land.

At this juncture I suppose it also bears mentioning that grandfather possessed a unique fondness for reading *The Classics,* as well as breeding quarter horses. Ergo my extensive library at home, as well as my equestrian savvy, which, when I borrowed the campus security guard's horse, came back to me, as they say... lickety-split.

Fulton University was known, among other things, as having an exceptional psychology department and the longest pedestrian bridge in the eastern part of the country. I didn't care all that much about the psychology department, other than, I suppose, using it as a springboard to publish a host of articles and treatises in the various medical books and journals that deemed them worthy – but the bridge? My lord, on a spring day, with the hemlock and fir in glorious bloom, the wind subtle, and the roar of the river announcing that it is finally free of the confining embrace of winter, it is a fine place to run an animal. Not because of the bridge, mind you – because once across it there are rolling green hills that seemingly go on forever.

Of course, forever comes to an end rather quickly when the police are waiting for you… as they were for me shortly after the horse and I galloped our way over.

Fortunately, the university did not press charges, not that I actually thought they would. In fact, my only punishment, beyond getting handcuffed and having to spend a couple of hours in the backseat of a patrol car, came in the form of a monotonous discussion with a longwinded, though fairly amused dean. Unfortunately, my wife did not share in the merriment, inclined, instead, to describe the situation as just another revealing episode of my *arrogant eccentricity,* a concept she favored when she was in an agreeable mood. Similar, I suppose, to those instances when she would depict my behavior as confusing – not embarrassing, improper – not irrational, misunderstood – not delusional – characterizations that frankly, I never paid all that much attention to.

I do not wish to imply that I did not care about and love my wife, however. I did… a couple of years back. She was a beautiful woman too, with radiant blue eyes, dark, finger-tussled hair that barely covered her slender shoulders, and skin as soft and smooth as a warm summer day.

In fact, we met on a warm summer day. I was riding my unicycle, which can be mighty interesting when you're casually flipping through the pages of a book, and she was walking toward me eating an ice cream cone. I thought little of the situation, and certainly never contemplated losing my balance, for riding unicycles was just like walking on my hands, another skill that I had become quite proficient at over the years, and yet, that is precisely what happened. I fell… rather, I crashed… into her. Neither of us was physically hurt, but I must admit, I felt more than a tad foolish because I ended up wearing the ice cream cone on my chin. That's correct, in the process of bumbling, stumbling, and tumbling over, Christina landed on me, I landed on the grass, and her ice cream cone came to rest on my chin, which, I don't mind telling you, turned into quite the sticky situation, what with the way it was melting down my throat and neck. Nevertheless, I managed to wink and, with a twisted smile strapped firmly in place, said, "If I don't take a shower for a couple of days my skin, particularly the area encompassing my chin, gets really oily and these strange looking things start growing out of it."

Well that did it, because no sooner did my light-hearted sarcasm take a spin through the air when she started to laugh, long and hard. I joined her, of course. I also joined her for dinner that night... as well as breakfast the following morning. In fact, it was during one of those many wonderful mornings when, after watching the sun break through the window only to dance upon her as though she were an angel of light, I finally admitted to myself what had to be so glaring to the rest of the free world – my face and body were no match for hers. How then... why then was she attracted to me? It was a question that jumped from my tongue the instant I jumped out of my bed.

"Because," she said, as though she had long anticipated the question, "in addition to the gentlest touch I've ever experienced and the softest, saddest pair of eyes I've ever looked into, you have a truly exquisite mind."

I do not know if I still possess a gentle touch, and I'm uncertain if my eyes remain a soft reflection of sad, but my truly exquisite mind did not last very long. In other words, a few years after we were married my escapades stretched far beyond Christina's comfort level. I do not believe there was any one event that caused this unfortunate circumstance. I did, however, first notice a change in my wife's behavior the night I spoke at Delaware Institute, the city's only private high school.

The students were fighting the imposition of a dress code and the school board president, Dr. Richard Samuel, a man I had come to know fairly well over the years, asked me to address all interested parties on what he described as, "The psychology underlying the mandate."

"Why me, Richard?" I asked. "I don't even believe in dress codes."

"I never assumed you did, Hub. But then, anyone who knows you knows of your tendency to test the waters... if you know what I mean?"

"Yes, I've heard those rumors," I replied, tongue-in-cheek. "Still, why do you think that what I have to say will carry your intended impact?"

"Because, Hub, those very rumors have made you a local celebrity of sorts."

"So?"

"So who better to speak on the dangers of fire than a popular fire victim?"

"But I don't consider myself a victim, Richard."

"Nor should you, Hub. But the kids don't know that. The only thing they'll know is that you, a man who has been known to dance to the beat of his drum, believe in the importance of structure and organization. So what do you say, you ready to pack the house?"

"I say rubbish, but if it means getting off the phone with you then fine. I'll do it. But you owe me one."

It turns out that my good friend the doctor was correct because every seat in every row of the auditorium was taken, leaving those without to clamor for a spot along the back wall. Thankfully, my speech didn't disappoint anyone. On the contrary, I received a long and thunderous standing ovation, particularly from the school board members, the faculty and the parents.

So why, you ask, did my wife's behavior begin to change that night? Simple, because once I finished my lecture and walked out from behind the podium, I took off the overcoat I was wearing and stood before the audience in nothing more than my shoes, socks, shirt, tie… and… *whoop-dee-do,* my boxer shorts; an ironic display of dress in light of my inspiring lecture on the importance of dress codes… wouldn't you say?

And therein lies the problem – Christina didn't say. Not about the lecture, the inflamed article in the local newspaper the following morning, or that I was asked to remove myself from consideration for the deanship of the psychology department at the university, a post I only mildly entertained because she implored me to. Rather, for the next few months Christina went about her business as though nothing had happened at all. At the time I just assumed she was either too preoccupied with motherhood, as we were the joyful parents of a lovely four-year-old girl named, Rita, or, simply found the entire matter too trivial to be bothered with. It never occurred to me that she suddenly viewed me as a *dangerously* troubled man. In fact, it was only after I took part in a debate concerning gay rights that I first realized the depths of her newfound opinion.

And no I am not gay. Nor have I ever been. I merely took part in a verbal jousting because an egregious crime against humanity had been committed.

On a harsh winter morning a young, local boy of fourteen had been found hanging from a tree. He had been beaten and stabbed... and oh yes, his penis had been cut off. A nomadic group of Hitler youths had been charged with the crime, but rather than admit their obvious and senseless guilt, they brought in one of their own, a lawyer who's name was Randolph Watkins, and whose appearance was that of a storm trooper. Not only did he promptly and proudly declare his clients' innocence, he petitioned, and won, the right to assemble on the courthouse steps to debate any man or woman on, what he termed, "The impurity in today's America."

It was an offer I could not resist. Nor, after thrashing this genetically flawed worm of an individual with facts, figures and, if I do say so myself, stunning brilliance, could I resist taking a swing (or two), at him. So I did, to the approving roar of the many people who had gathered in attendance.

Unfortunately, the legal system saw it differently. You see, I was wearing makeup and a dress. I was also carrying a purse, which is what I used to smack Randolph Watkins with. I was not dressed this way to cause a disturbance or diminish the severity of the issues at hand. On the contrary, I simply wanted Mr. Watkins to be publicly humiliated by the very type of individual he was seeking to condemn. Yet, I was the one humiliated as I was arrested for disturbing the peace and assault and battery – charges that saw me spend a night in jail, only to stand in open court the following day (in full dress regalia, including purse), and have a female judge tell me, after so graciously handing me a two year probationary period, that I was making a mockery of women everywhere.

As for my wife... she didn't view my actions as a mockery toward women anymore than she viewed them an effective approach to shedding new light on an old problem. Instead, Christina determined my methods to be those of a man whose existence is dependent solely upon the evolving absurdity of the very situations he incites. "Worst of all," she insisted, "you won't stop until there's no way out – until you're dead, locked up in jail, or locked away inside your own childish insanity. And you know why? Because you have a void that cannot be filled. You just don't know it, that's your problem."

Of course I responded by telling my wife there is no such thing as childish insanity, to which she promptly countered, "Don't pull that psychiatry crap with me. You're a child and you're insane. So as far as I'm concerned you suffer from childish insanity."

Yes, well, I never thought of myself as a child, and I've certainly never thought of myself as insane. True, I've had occasion to question some of my exploits, but only when the relevant situation turned out differently than what I might have anticipated, not because my efforts were impelled by some misguided silliness or some maddening disease of the mind.

Nevertheless, according to Christina my troubling behavior was seriously threatening our marriage.

I didn't respond right then, languishing instead over the notion that those episodic adventures which first attracted my wife to, what she called my, "truly exquisite mind," were now doing just the opposite. What changed, I wondered? And did it matter? Of the former I can only guess time, space and the tolerance between. Of the latter, my god, with a beautiful daughter I so dearly loved and cherished – yes, yes, yes, it mattered! Like oxygen, it mattered! Therefore, I had but one choice... to do as Christina insisted and make an appointment with Dr. Sherman Wilkes, a twice-divorced marriage counselor.

I know, a twice-divorced marriage counselor sounds utterly ridiculous to me as well, but, since he was rumored to be a brilliant savior, this, according to Christina's pretentious group of nosy friends, and, since perception is nine/tenths of the law, this, according to me, what could I do, but go? So I did. Actually we, Christina and I, both went to see this fine, upstanding doctor. Quite a handsome gent to be sure. A finely tailored face, he sported a perfectly even tan, possessed a flowing crop of black hair (tinted gray at the temples of course), spoke in soft, eloquent tones, and apparently enjoyed smiling, for both his green eyes and white teeth sparkled quite often.

Interestingly enough, I'm not sure what he found so amusing. I suppose he could have been entertained by a few of my escapades, although Christina never told a story that wasn't laced with a solid dose of the humdrum, especially when she retraced every infinitesimal detail just to underscore her *correct* point of view. Therefore my reasoning was a fragile assumption at best. Of course, as long as I was committed to pacifying, what I sincerely believed to be my wife's well intentioned, but misguided course-of-action, what difference did his reason for smiling really make?

None – although, strangely enough I had a deep-seated desire to know. As such, the moment Christina was excused from our session, the good doctor having determined that it would be better if he and I spoke alone, I said, "Dr. Wilkes, I certainly don't mean to interrupt your train of thought – heaven knows, I have my fair share of interruptions – but I'm curious about something?"

"Yes, what is it Dr. Webster? How can I help you?" He returned, the question basking in the glow of his ever-present smile.

"Well, since I don't wish to envision myself, or my situation as a basis for your comic relief, I must know... why in god's name are you constantly smiling?"

Dr. Wilkes fidgeted in his seat for a couple of moments before telling me that his condition, though not intentional, was the result of a facelift gone astray.

"Interesting," I said, smiling myself at the prospect of getting a little too much nip and tuck with your nip and tuck.

Dr. Wilkes shrugged. I don't know, I've thought about having them fix it, but..."

"But what?"

Dr. Wilkes grabbed hold of the mirror on his desk, filled it with a lingering starry-eyed gaze, and then said, "I have a really nice smile. I mean a *really, really* nice smile. I find that it helps brighten people's moods, which is worth its weight in gold because moods can get pretty bleak around here. It's one of the many tools I use. Another happens to be my hands. Look at them, they're beautifully manicured. And boy, are they soft. So soft, in fact, I have couples hold them in their own hands – you know to get a sense of the very warmth they're looking for from each other. And if that doesn't work, though it seldom fails, I hug my patients. First the women so they get an accurate feel for what it's like to be held by a strong pair of arms, and then the men, so they get an accurate understanding of how it feels to the woman."

"You don't say?"

"Ah, but I do say. And if none of that works, well then, let's just say I've been known to teach the men about stroking their wives. Their hair, their arms... you get the idea, don't you?"

"Wonderful techniques, Doctor, wonderful techniques," I said, the acerbity in my voice humming at full throttle.

"Would you like me to show you? I could..."

"No, no, that's fine. I understand everything perfectly."

"Okay, but that's not all of it, Dr. Webster."

"You're kidding, there's more?" I asked, tossing my hands to my cheeks.

"Yes, when all else fails, I instruct my clients on the importance of helping their partners release pressure. I show them various points on the body, the underside of the foot, the nape of the neck, the lower part of the back. Massaging, squeezing, all of it designed to release pressure, all of it to help them get in touch with one another. You sure you don't want me to demonstrate. I can just…"

"No, no, like I said, I'm perfectly fine. A demonstration, in fact, might just be more than I can bear right now."

"Perhaps, perhaps not. Either way you can visualize just how extensive the benefits might be, can't you?"

"Oh absolutely, absolutely," I replied, as I got up from my chair and headed for the door. "Not only that, I can also see, I mean *really, really* see why you have a reputation as a brilliant savior."

"What do you mean?" Dr. Wilkes asked.

"Well, quite frankly, I mean so long, goodbye, and *toodaloo*."

Convinced that my *inappropriate behavior* was the underlying reason we were no longer welcome at the office of Dr. Sherman Wilkes, marriage counselor extraordinaire, Christina returned to her silence. In fact, beyond obligatory discussions concerning our daughter, Rita, she did not speak to me for several days on end. It was a difficult time too, as I suddenly found myself trapped between what was quickly becoming Christina's emotional sterility, and my own deeply rooted sense of self. Would I… could I ever live my life with the same carefree wisdom that somehow brought me this far? Or, was the possibility of everyday life without the face of my daughter to look at as genuine as Christina wanted me to believe? Questions I did not wish to answer…which, of course, was the answer itself. I would delay this confrontation as long as I could by agreeing to see another marriage counselor.

Christina did not warm to the idea, however, until I once again acquiesced to her choice of doctor.

Stewart Baines, a marriage counselor never-before-married (a strange concept to fathom, I readily admit), was a sturdy looking fellow. Not necessarily large, but between his square jaw and broad shoulders he filled his chair quite differently than the slightly built Sherman Wilkes. He also sported a small scar just under the creases of his right eye, which, when coupled with his lightly whiskered face, lead me to believe that he had no immediate plans to become a poster boy for cosmetic surgery. The combination did, however, give him a ruggedly handsome look, an appearance furthered strengthened by his deliberate, but raspy speech.

Dr. Baines did share one ingredient with Sherman Wilkes, however. They both preferred meeting with Christina and I together, as well as the two of us individually. Was it an effective method of practice? Who can say? More importantly why did Dr. Baines feel the need to solicit my approval on the matter? Even when I suggested my uncertainty he pressed on, telling me that until such time as I was convinced, he would be unable to assist Christina and me in our efforts to resuscitate our marital bond.

Splendid, I thought. Exorcise the patient's freedom of thought. Coerce blind allegiance under a guise of futility. Introduce the fragility of a crumbling marriage to the rigidity of programmed treatment. *Make them listen, make them listen, make them listen! Never change, never change, never change! You are right, you are right, you are right! They will improve, they will improve, they will improve! Never change, never change, never change!*

Yes, well, far be it from me to express my real concerns, especially since my *exceedingly cautious* wife was convinced before she even walked through the door. Alas, what's a confused husband to do when the only clarity in his life is his love for the child born to him by the woman sitting to his left?

And so began our weekly sessions with Dr. Stewart Baines. Sessions that belittled my wayward style of dress as just another means to garner attention – sessions that determined my *reckless behavior* to be little more than my inability to harness, or, at a minimum, channel my brazen energy – sessions that sought to explore every intimate detail of the once divine sex life I shared with my wife, Christina – sessions that some three months after they began, Dr. Baines abruptly announced would end. "Your continued reluctance to embrace personal change has handcuffed us all," he declared. "It's not fair to your marriage, to your wife, or, for that matter, to me. Frankly, Dr. Webster, you and your obstinacy need something besides me – a psychiatrist, perhaps... one other than yourself. And should you get help at some point and want to try this again, let me know and we'll see. Until that day, however, I can no longer be of service."

So there I was, out in the proverbial cold once again. In fact, had it not been for my daughter Rita, my lovely Rita, I would have felt like an aimless shadow in my own house, for my wife, Christina, *"repulsed at the very thought of me, sickened by the very sight of me,"* withdrew into a world of her own. A world defined by the haughty sparkle of a social calendar, the cavalier nurturing of a suddenly inconvenient child, and the cold, calloused walls of a separate bedroom. Yes, I was indeed deeply saddened by the poignant turn of events. I was not, however, so despondent that I failed to recognize the wonderful gifts that my little girl bestowed upon me – hope, meaning, and, perhaps for the first time in my life, a lucid perception of myself.

Rita gave me something else, as well; a playful companion to stroll the sandy beaches along the Atlantic (where we spent many a Sunday morning chasing seagulls and building sandcastles), the boutiques along Mill Avenue (where, after frolicking in the dew laden countryside of my late grandfather, we would often stop for ice cream), and the apple orchards north of Hastings (a personal favorite because I found great pleasure in watching my daughter fumble around in her efforts to extract apples from trees).

Yet, in all our splendid time together, there is perhaps one single moment that I shall forever cherish. It was the day I gave Rita a pony for her fifth birthday. Her mother, as had been the norm for almost a year, preferred to mingle with friends rather than celebrate something besides herself – an afternoon of superfluous shopping, a weekend of pamper and frivolous travel, a cocktail party, a dinner party… anywhere I wasn't invited and a dress code was employed. Of course, I, in turn, could not have been happier, for Christina's recurring absence gave me more uninterrupted time with Rita than I could have ever hoped for.

In truth, my plan did not call for the purchase of a pony. However, in light of my marital strife, the catalyst for what had become a continuing effort on my part to take stock of my life, I deemed it necessary to embrace my past. Most notably the summers spent on my grandfather's farm, for aside from the time spent with my daughter, they represented, unequivocally, the most gratifying times in my life. So yes, when I first saw the pony I was instantly reminded of the day my grandfather walked me inside his corral, his leathery palm gently squeezing the back of my neck, where, not twenty yards away, stood a magnificent looking animal. Snowy white mane atop rich black skin, his head bounced up and down, as though greeting my presence. And then, in a flash, he broke to his right, darted effortlessly to his left, and then broke back the other way, where he came to an abrupt stop, looked at me, and bounced his head once more.

"What do you want to call him?" My grandfather asked.

"I don't know, what do you?" I countered.

"Well," grandfather announced, "since it's your horse, you get to choose."

That may very well have been the first time in my life where I was left speechless. In fact, beyond hugging my grandfather with all the strength I could possibly muster, I stood in wondrous disbelief, graced by the spirit of both a beautiful animal, and the beautiful man who gave him to me.

For what it's worth, I named my horse, Sequoia, in honor of a great Cherokee scholar that I had read about as a child. More importantly, I named my daughter, Rita, in honor of my grandfather, Rennie, an exquisite man, who, to this day, I still think about. And as I watched my daughter marvel at the splendor of her new pony, I saw the likeness of his face in hers and my eyes grew moist. Of course, as soon as Rita leapt into my arms and told me how much she loved me, the tears I had been able to contain broke free.

Yes, well, it was several months before I heard my daughter speak those lovely words again, for less than a week after Rita and I celebrated her birthday, I returned home one night to complete emptiness… save for an old card table, a twin bed from one of the two guest bedrooms, a handful of chinaware, and my books (thankfully). Much to my dismay, my wife, you see, had not spent *all* her time gallivanting from one trivial happening to the next as I had so mistakenly believed. On the contrary, according to the letter she left for me on my *new* dining-room table, she had been setting up house… with Dr. Stewart Baines, no less. Christina further mentioned that she had filed for divorce, this, the result of my *potentially dangerous transgressions,* was planning to seek full custody of our daughter, this, the result of my *potentially dangerous transgressions,* and, had removed the vast majority of our joint savings, this (although she didn't say), the result of her wanton greed.

Nevertheless, I had the value of my grandfather's estate to depend on... and that is precisely what I did in order to hire the finest lawyer I could find. Yet, and notwithstanding the simple premise that I was truly distraught by the chilling turn of events, I did not desire reconciliation with my wife. Nor was I concerned about the household furniture, the money, or that she was living with Dr. Stewart Baines, circumstances that her lawyer said had everything to do with fear and absolutely nothing to do with a desire to cohabitate. (And I, of course, fell out of a tree and landed on my head at an early age).

That said, my one and only desire was to regain custody of Rita. As a result, I instructed my attorney, Mr. William Stark, of *Stark, Chalmers and Stark,* to do everything in his power to see the situation through. "No matter the cost, I do not want my daughter exposed to the baseless virtues of her mother anymore than I want her living under the same roof with that unethical and shameless bastard of a man."

"I'll do everything I can," Mr. Stark assured me.

Yes, well assurances aside, my case was unfortunately assigned to Judge Wilma Stevens, the same obtuse judge who put me on probation for assaulting that insidious Nazi lawyer after I battered him in what turned out to be an unrewarding debate on the courthouse steps. At any rate, she did not find my transgressions to be *potentially dangerous.* She did, however, find that I was not a suitable candidate for custodial parent, reducing my parental stake to visitation rights – once a week and every other weekend to be exact.

I was incredulous, to say the least. In fact, I sprang from my seat and demanded an answer. "How is that possible... how?" I fumed. "Is your mindset so predisposed that you're oblivious to the unscrupulous shenanigans of my pitiful wife and her lover... a man who I dare say will be brought before the medical ethics committee by the time I'm finished?"

Judge Stevens simply exhaled her pompous attitude, and said, "It's your personal history, Dr. Webster, nothing more."

Suffice it to say, after appealing the judge's ruling, to no avail, mind you, I was left with little choice but to make the very most of the short time Rita and I were allowed to spend together. Yet, we picked up right where we left off... chasing seagulls, picking apples, and, by all means, visiting with her pony, who, as I explained to my little girl, would be moving to a new stall just as soon as construction was completed. Shortly after the divorce, you see, I decided to build a country-style home on a beautiful two-hundred-fifty acre parcel of land that once belonged to my grandfather – land, you may recall, that I repurchased out of proceeds from his estate. Over the last several years I had actually been able to repurchase close to six hundred acres. Yet, not all the land was contiguous. Therefore, I chose the parcel most compatible for horses. And while it would be many months before the entire project was finished, upon completion there would a generous size home, a corral large enough to accommodate three to four dozen horses, a riding stable for Rita to learn proper technique, and, most importantly, enough wide open space to run, as they say… lickety-split.

Sadly enough, a single phone call from Christina brought my grand venture to a screeching halt.

"It's all your fault!" She screamed, the moment I put the receiver to my ear. "All your fault! If you hadn't gone after Stew, none of this would have happened!"

"Calm down, calm down," I implored. "I don't even know what you're talking about. What's happened?"

"Rita, she's been hurt."

"Hurt, what do you mean hurt? When? How bad?"

"She's in the hospital," Christina replied between sobs. "And it's your fault."

"What happened, damn-it? What happened?" I asked, my body trembling beyond measure.

"The malpractice grievance you filed against Stew. The medical board acted on it. They've suspended his license."

"Christina, I'm going to ask you one more time," I stated, the words barely able to escape my clenched teeth. "And if you don't answer me then so help me god I'm going to come over there and ring it out of you. Now, what happened to my daughter?"

Christina sighed before responding, "Stew beat her up. He was mad because of what you did."

"He did what?" I roared. "Where is he? Tell me where he is!"

"He left the house, I don't know where. And I'm still at the hospital so I don't know if he's gone back home."

"What about Rita, how is she?" I asked, my fury all but overwhelming my ability to hold still for an answer.

Christina sighed again. "The doctor said she's going to be fine. But..."

"But what?" I bellowed.

"She's suffered a broken arm. And her face..."

"What about her face, Christina? What about her face?"

Christina did not reply, and I no longer cared if she did. At that moment I only had room for two glaring thoughts: The welfare of my daughter, and the deranged man who jeopardized it.

As it turned out, Stewart Baines did indeed return home that evening, where, upon opening his front door, I unleashed a rage I never knew I possessed. I've often heard it referred to as *father's rage*. Still, having never studied the subject matter I cannot say with any degree of authority. What I can say, however, is that I pummeled Stewart Baines until both his arms were broken and his rugged good looks were reduced to an unrecognizable pool of red.

Of course, that is merely the beginning of the story's end. Stewart Baines, you see, in addition to losing his medical license for six *long and arduous* months, was handed a *whopping* one year prison term. According to the illustrious Judge Wilma Stevens, (oh yes, between my divorce and previous probation she retained jurisdiction over my person), punishment was minimized because, in addition to having a perfectly clean record Stewart Baines owned a reputation as an exemplary citizen of the community – which, in the predictable scheme of things, meant that he would soon be the proud owner of freedom... as he was paroled some five months later.

I, on the other hand, was not the recipient of such propitious treatment. On the contrary, after I stood in open court (having been charged with breaking the terms of said probation, as well as intent to commit bodily harm), and shamelessly admitted the barbaric facts, Judge Stevens said, "Your personal history, Dr. Webster, your strange behavior, it's all such a shame. From everything I've either heard or read, you've shown flashes of absolute brilliance, but brilliance is no excuse for behavior that is so unpredictable, so scurrilous. Quite frankly, I'm afraid you're capable of hurting someone else... perhaps even yourself. Therefore, I have no choice but to confine you to

Valley View Mental Institution until I'm properly convinced you're no longer a danger to anyone."

And there you have it... at the drop of a hollow gavel the sum total of my existence reduced to observation and speculation, deductive reasoning and estimation, interrogation and cerebration, inkblots... and if I'm lucky all the turkey hash I can gobble down, at the one... the only... venerable and vine-covered Valley View Mental Institution.

Where I remain to this day.

The Green, Green Grass of Home

Summer is barely over, and though winter feels like it's only a mile or two away, there's still enough time to walk barefooted along the narrow ridge that joins the evergreen and the bitterroot. Depending on where I stand, or the direction I look, I can see for what seems like a thousand miles, my vision corralled only by the weakness of my eyes and the strength of the sunlight's glare. Nevertheless, with the lush green valley before me, the expansive blue sky above me, and the rich smell of pine cones and wild flowers to fill the air, I know that where I am is second to no other place on earth.

As a boy, sure-footed and swift, I took for granted the splendor of my surroundings and the games I played within. Freedom was not an issue, the pursuit of happiness was achieved everyday it didn't rain, and my life was protected under a sovereignty of justice.

As an adult I've naturally changed. My movement is slower, more deliberate. I now take stock in splendor wherever I can find it, and games are generally played when I have the time, money and inclination. Freedom, however, still is not an issue, the pursuit of happiness, as always, is a worthier endeavor when skies are sunny, and my life remains protected under a sovereignty of justice.

At what cost, however, has this sovereignty of justice, this backdrop of peace and democracy, this stage where the sum of our rights are absolute, and we, as a people, remain exempt from restraint of thought and movement, come?

The casualties lost in the many wars fought embody the answer to that question far better than the handful of words I could ever come up with. Suffice it to say we would not celebrate our history as a nation but for the immeasurable sacrifices made by the men and women who have gone before us. Nor would our country have ever positioned itself as leader of the free world. Perhaps the better question entails the cost Americans will endure in order that our liberties endure.

We stand at a time in history when the face of mankind is scarred by the filth of terrorism – when the sanctity of life is marred by man's inhumanity to man – when prayer is worshipped by followers of hatred and deceit – when leadership is defined by utter madness – and, when the eve of destruction is but a holy war away.

Holy war. The world dangles from its tightening noose and I, for one, don't even know what it is. I can make sense of the Holy Bible, Holy Communion, Holy Cross, Holy Father, Holy Ghost, Holy Grail, Holy City, Holy Bread, Holy Water, Holy Land and Holy Day. Come to think of it, I can even make sense out of Holy Moses, Holy Roller, Holy Cow, Holy Smoke and Holy Mackerel. I just can't get a grip on holy war. To tell you the truth, if I had to put my best *holy-war-foot-forward,* I'd probably describe it as the quintessential contradiction in terms and let it go at that.

Let's be honest – if holy encompasses that which is sacred and spiritually pure then it must be untainted by evil and sin. War, on the other hand, is the venom of evil and sin. Therefore, it is difficult, and if it were not so pathetic, comical as well, to think of holy war as *sacred evil,* or *spiritually pure sin.*

Now consider the term, holy shit, or, as the case may be, the discharge of *spiritually pure excrement.* I ask you, how can something so spiritually pure smell so sinfully awful? In my mind, it cannot. Moreover, because the purity in each instance is comprised of adulterating matter, I think it's fair to say that there is a conceptual similarity between the two – one that spawns the argument that *holy war* and *holy shit* are cut from the same *holy cloth.* In other words, *the declaration of holy war is, in reality, the act of taking a holy shit.*

That said, I also don't understand the quest for martyrdom; what has become a much ballyhooed byproduct of holy war. Does not martyrdom assume the state of self-sacrifice in the face of compromising principles and beliefs? Is it not the acceptance of fate and pain before the deprivation of faith and cause? And if so, how does that translate into murdering innocent people? How does driving a bus into a group of school children, blowing up a house of worship, crashing a jetliner into a building, or, frankly, setting off a bomb wherever and whenever possible, regardless of the lives at stake – how is that the acceptance of fate and pain before the deprivation of faith and cause, when, in fact, the only pain suffered is by the family of the murdered victims, and the only deprivation has been of the innocent lives taken?

Perhaps the answer lies in the premise… there are no innocent victims in the throes of holy war. Holy war is waged in the name of god against anyone who does not subscribe to that particular brand of holiness. Therefore, those who die are supposed to. Of course, for this to occur we have to believe that god both decrees and condones the taking of human life. It's either that, in which case the god some of us have believed in all these years is a little more screwed up than we previously thought, or, there's another god roaming the heavens out there. Unfortunately, that turns the situation into a, *my god is better than your god* scenario. Need I say more?

Actually it's not a proposition in need of a response, for terrorism is not about god. It's about repudiating capitalism, even though terrorists are the first to use capitalistic tools to fund their heinous acts. It's about obliterating the spirit of democracy, celebrating instead, a repugnant form of government, one replete with all the oppression, corruption and bloodshed of a typically uneducated and contemptible nazi state. It's about denying the same basic human rights that our country seeks to provide and protect, both at home and abroad. It's about killing the sanctity of America's freedom and her cherished way of life.

And now, as I continue to walk barefooted along the narrow ridge that joins the evergreen and the bitterroot, the insidious face of terrorism trying to block my view, I momentarily close my eyes – opening them, only to scan the rolling green fields that stretch from my feet to the arms of the Rocky Mountains. It is then when I hear the song, America the Beautiful, whistling through the crisp autumn air.

Robert Edward Levin

Letters from Home

Wrote a letter to my oldest boy, Davey Jr., today. Second time this month. He didn't answer my other letter, but since I wasn't of a mind to call him, I figured I'd write him again. Probably won't do me a lick of good, though. I've been writin' him letters for the last ten years and only got one in return. And that one wasn't very long at that. Couple of paragraphs to be exact. Now you'd think bein' his father would warrant somethin' more than a couple of measly ol' paragraphs, but uh-uh, it didn't.

I didn't much care for what it said either. Bunch of silly nonsense 'bout wantin' to be left alone. Wantin' to find his own way without havin' to worry 'bout me barkin' at him all the time. Told me I'm always tryin' to change his direction. Said he's tired of hearin' me squawk about the size of my shoes, or, that every time he starts doin' good at somethin' the size of my shoes grow.

It's true, that boy's got a long way to go before he ever catches up to me. Unfortunately, his biggest problem is gonna be stayin' out of his own way. I mean, no matter what he does, there always seems to be a better way of doin' things. Now I admit, when he was growin' up there were times, more than a few, in fact, when I wasn't quite sure how to approach a situation myself. So just to be on the safe side what I'd do is, I'd let him run with things long enough to make sure his course of action was indeed wrong before pointin' it out. Naturally, I'd also point out what obviously turned out to be the correct way (my way), of handlin' the situation.

It ain't like I was tryin' to hurt his feelings, or anything. I just figured it was more important that I be right than it was to spare him a hurtful moment or two. Let's face it, how else am I gonna set an example for the boy if me, his father, can't be right? The thing is, Davey Jr. never saw it quite the same way, so after awhile I gave up tryin' to teach him. Instead, I just started directin' him to, *"Follow my lead, son! Follow my lead!"* He never followed, though. Didn't matter if I instructed him to do so in private, in front of his friends, brothers and sister, mother... anybody for that matter. Hell, he'd just stick his head inside a book, hide out in his room, or offer up an opinion that was a whole lot different than mine.

Can you imagine? A little snot-nosed kid who never had the gumption to get dirt under his fingernails havin' the nerve to give me his opinion on what's right, wrong, true, false, good, bad, big, small, black, white, or even red? I can't imagine it, that's for sure. More importantly, I never hesitated a single second before correctin' him. I'd say, "Davey Jr., face facts. It ain't that I'm smarter; you just don't have my good sense, no matter how many books you stick your nose in. It ain't that all my hard work proved me to be a better man, you're just too busy lookin' for yourself to prove much of anything."

Funny thing about it, to this day I don't know if Davey Jr. ever found himself. Like I said, he don't write me anymore.

Wrote a letter to my second oldest boy, Stevie Ray, today. Stevie Ray, he's a pretty good kid, even though I ain't heard from him in almost six years. And even then he just dropped me a line to tell me he was livin' in Iowa, not too far from his older brother. Of course listenin' to Davey Jr. has always been one of Stevie Ray's biggest problems. Especially since Davey was always tellin' him to keep a safe distance from me – somethin' 'bout bein' bad for the spirit, bad for the backbone. Said that tryin' to please me was a never-endin' and useless goal for anybody – that Stevie Ray should look to make his own mark on the world.

Now people, Davey Jr. included, can say whatever they want to about me, but one thing's for sure, I've never done a goddamn thing to anybody's spirit or backbone. Especially Stevie Ray. The fact is I always encouraged him to be more active in sports simply b'cuz he had all the trappings of a real man. Even when he wasn't showin' the proper interest I kept pushin' him, knowin' full well that it was for his own good, his own backbone, if you will. Lord knows he had the talent. Not near as much as I did when I was his age (which I made sure to point out whenever he seemed light on motivation), but he weren't half-bad.

And then one day he came home and said he wasn't playin' ball anymore. Said I could call him a sissy all I wanted, it wouldn't make a bit of difference. Evidently it didn't b'cuz I called him Sissy Ray 'stead of Stevie Ray in front of one and all for an entire year and all he'd do is stare at the floor.

All that aside, however, Stevie Ray's biggest problem has always been his wife. He met her just after graduatin' high school, which, coincidentally enough, just happened to be about the time I started to lose control of the boy. It's not that givin' up control was so bad (especially since I had a couple more kids at home), it's just that whenever I tried givin' him some advise or helpin' him out in some capacity, my god, that wife of his would look at me and all but explode. "Haven't you done enough to him already?" She'd ask, her voice rushin' at me like the bullets from a shotgun. "Can't you just leave him alone?"

I dunno, maybe if I was doin' somethin' bad to the boy I would've considered lettin' him be. But I never did a thing. In fact, the only one to ever hurt him, aside from Davey Jr., of course, was his wife. And that was the moment she started chewin' on his ear about movin' out of town and goin' to college, as if a college education, good as it is, will ever give him the intelligence that hard work has given me. No, I don't see how movin' away from me, the only positive influence that boy has ever had, is beneficial at all. I tell him so in every letter I write to him too.

But frankly, I don't know what he thinks. Like I said, Stevie Ray don't write me anymore.

Wrote a letter to my only daughter, Emily, today. Boy, talk about a good-looker. I even asked her in my latest letter if she's still as pretty as she used to be. Of course, since she hasn't dropped me a line in almost four years, and even then only to tell me to stay away from her and the kids, her continued good looks is just somethin' I'll have to assume.

Sure wish it were different. Sure wish she hadn't run off with that husband of hers. Goes by the name of Tom Madison, or, pardon me, Dr. Thomas Madison. Either way he ain't a very likable fella. I mean, the first few times I met him I tried to take him under my wing, just like all my boys, but he refused my efforts. I guess bein' a doctor means he's too good for me. Anyway, since life ain't supposed to be lived in the shadow of somebody else's ego, I decided to ignore him altogether. Not that I cared, mind you. In fact, I told Emily the only thing I cared about were her and her kids. That's why for the life of me I can't understand why she'd ask me to stay away.

But Emily, she's always been a strange one. I mean, I never saw a person so hell-bent on pleasin' somebody get so discouraged so quickly. But that's how she was. One minute she'd be racin' down the stairs to tell me about her report card – "Look daddy, look how good I did" – the next minute, after I'd get done explainin' to her that she could've done better, she'd be mopin' around like she just lost her little kitty. Hell, I even remember the time when she was nominated for Homecoming Queen in her high school class. She carried a smile from ear to ear. Yet, when the family was all gathered around the dinner table and I explained to her that bein' nominated don't mean a damn thing if ya don't win (figurin' I was teachin' her one of life's little lessons), that smile of hers turned into a bucket of tears.

Now if actions like that don't smack of strange behavior, well then, I remember the time when she came home with news about getting her first teaching job. There she was with a big proud sparkle in her eyes, braggin' and carryin' on to anybody with a pair of ears, when I said, "Yeah, that's nice honey, but until you get a job as a college professor, bein' a teacher ain't really that big a deal." And suddenly, that big proud sparkle turned into a scowl and all that braggin' and whatnot turned into a weeklong hiss.

Of course, none of that stuff has anything to do with why she wants me to stay away from her kids. Unfortunately, she won't give me her exact reasoning. Like I said, Emily, she don't write me anymore.

Wrote a letter to my ex-wife, Lydia, today. It's the first one this month. We got divorced right about the time our last child moved out of the house. Anyway, I was just writing her to see how she was getting along, if she needed any money… that sort of thing.

Lydia, you see, wouldn't take a plug nickel from me in the divorce. Said she just wanted a fresh start. Said she planned to go back to work, be it as a secretary, sellin' women's clothes, didn't really matter. But that ain't the half of it. After I told her that being a secretary or sellin' clothes were both measly jobs, she said she also planned to go back to school, community college to be exact. Didn't know what kind of degree she wanted, hoped to figure it out somewhere along the way.

"Now what the hell could somebody like you possibly get out of college?" I asked her, in no uncertain terms. "You ain't no student. Hell, about the only thing you've ever done in your life is cook, clean, and be a mother. But now, with all our kids gone, you won't even have to do that. Why then would you pick a time like this to get a

Robert Edward Levin

divorce? A time we could be spendin' together without so much as a sneeze of an interruption between us?"

Lydia didn't bother answering. She just shook her head, smiled, and walked out of the house.

The next time I saw my wife was in court. It also happened to be the last time that I saw her. In fact, if she hadn't sent me a letter with her forwarding address I wouldn't have known where to send the rest of her clothes. Not only that, I wouldn't know where to mail my letters to.

Although I'm not sure it matters because Lydia, she don't write me anymore.

I'd write a letter to my youngest boy, Red, but he killed himself a few years back. Didn't leave a note. Just left himself dangling from a rope. Nice kid, he was. Didn't talk a helluva lot and had a bad habit of leavin' a room as soon as I walked in it. But a nice kid just the same.

Yep, I'd write him if there were some point in it, but since there ain't, I'll just sit back in my rocking chair and listen to its lonely whine crawl along the dusty floors of this drafty old house.

Time

(The abridged version)

Time... 'tis a strange thing. It has no agenda, but to pass, and yet, its passing is often ignored, but for the parade of events that we personalize, emphasize, and, unfortunately, dramatize – such, that we don't hear the steps of its sure-footed march forward, until, of course, it is oft times, too late. Or, if it is not too late, if some horrid event hits so close to home that we suddenly embrace time as the cherished commodity it is, the situation only lasts until our mind's eye no longer recognizes the very fear that gave rise to it in the first place. Yet, it is during the course of this recognition when we are prone to experience a change in attitude, one that generally leans toward the sobriety of reflection or the spontaneity of *carpe diem, ('seize the day')*.

Of reflection, there seems to be a rebirth of moralities, characterized best, perhaps, by the immediate and systematic realignment of our principles – principles that until the moment of reflection may not have been any more steadfast than what the circumstances dictated at the time. Still, the realignment does suggest transgressions of the past, or, if not transgressions, than at least some belief that there is a need for behavioral change.

Is it a weakness to adjust our principles? This would obviously depend on the principles themselves, but in all likelihood, probably not. If there is a weakness, it is likely manifested in the simple premise that but for some horrid event, but for the sobriety of reflection, brought about only because there has been a sudden realization that the sure-footed march of time can end for anybody – at anytime – we would not have entertained the need for any personal adjustment at all.

That said, is the concept, *carpe diem* any different? Sure, it's different from a reactionary standpoint, but if it stems solely from a *here today, gone tomorrow* circumstance, such that we have made the conscious decision to take control of the moment and live only for the present, then how resolute is the motive that drives this sudden change in attitude? Of course, if our lust for instant gratification does not harm others then given the freedom to live life as one sees fit, I'm not certain motive is all that important.

What seems far more essential is making a concerted effort to harness a steady appreciation of time (regardless of the underlying reason provoking it).

Time: A finite series of events; the sequential relations that any event has to any other; the absolute duration standing between life and death. Yet, if there is to be a finite series of events, shouldn't we, in order to recognize the duration that stands between our own life and death try to grasp, try to appreciate the sequential relations that inconsequential events posses? In other words, can we afford to overlook, or take for granted, the finite incidents of daily life because we are all too consumed with getting to a more dramatic point in our lives? By the same token, can we afford to cast a blind eye in the direction of some future and dramatic point all because we are too consumed with maximizing every moment of the present? To the latter I say yes… assuming, of course, I have been given an endless bank account and the promise, by no less than God himself that I will happily live to be one hundred and fifty years old. Aside from that gloriously self-serving, preposterous notion, however, I don't think so. I don't think I could realistically live by the adage, *No time like the present!* I don't have enough faith in my abilities to ward off the excesses that would most certainly follow. And if I could not ward off such excesses, then how, pragmatically speaking, am I going to survive, much less appreciate time?

Unfortunately, I don't find the alternative scenario any less challenging. That is to say, if I can so willingly forget, discount, or flat-out ignore the finite series of events that fall between where I am and where I want to be, then what justice have I served upon myself? Is it not my role as a human being to explore the various elements of life, if by so doing I will be challenged by the diversities they bring, in turn affording me the opportunity to become a richer, fuller person? Yet, how can this be accomplished if I don't take the time necessary to be challenged by the attributes of the present?

I'm not talking about taking the time to *smell the roses* here. In fact, in my particular case I am somehow strangely allergic to roses so I make every effort to avoid them. I'm talking about backing off from the incessant pursuit of the future. For just as sure I am that living only for the here and now presents the potential for dangerously narcissistic tendencies, I am equally sure that living only with a mind on tomorrow would leave us with exactly that… a mind on tomorrow.

Not today, not yesterday... simply tomorrow, which, translated, means, *we can't wait to get "there"* (wherever *"there"* is). I also can't help but think, at least in the abstract sense, that such a quality makes us grandparents before parents and parents before kids.

Something else... what happens if we do get to this place, this bountiful station in life, and realize upon our arrival that we are still unfulfilled, that there is yet another destination to reach? That suddenly, and without warning, the place we have given every conceivable thought to was, alas, just another stepping stone to someplace else? Would we then lend every conceivable thought to this new journey? Would this new journey, this new matter-of-fact goal of ours be our last? Of this I am not sure, although I must confess: I find nothing wrong with the evolution of personal goals, for they provide a necessary and stable ingredient for personal growth, without which we could not perpetuate our own wellbeing.

However, I do not think such is the case when, in pursuit of a goal, we allow our unfettered, single-mindedness to circumvent our appreciation for the sequential relations of events in the living of our daily lives. It presents a situation, perhaps more than any other, that will inevitably cause us to peer over our respective shoulders one day, realize the setting sun's long and empty shadow is drawing ever so close, and ask, *"Where n' the hell did the time go?"*

An interesting question? I suppose. An unfortunate question would seem far more appropriate, because once it is asked it is often times too late to do anything about it. Yet, maybe that's why we run to the doctor for a little nip and tuck, which may indeed tighten an age line or posture a younger looking breast, but otherwise remains little more than a hopeless water stain from the fountain of youth. By the same token, maybe that's why we befriend the handful of memories we've managed to collect over the years, because like the nip and tuck, we become sufficiently indulged in the comfort they bring and in the escape they provide. On the other hand, maybe that's why we ultimately seek absolution, both from ourselves and from our sins.

In any event, when all is said and done nothing and no one can diminish the ominous reality we will no doubt feel once we come to grips with the profound notion that time, or, more appropriately, the end of time, is rapidly approaching.

And what of this imperiled state of being? Will we tiptoe through what time we have left, outfitted in all the trappings of poetic lore, and offer as we go, the unique and prophetic understanding of the daily life we forgot to live?

I don't know. I truly don't. Perhaps if we actually live it, however, we won't feel so compelled to.

The Story of Nick

Thirty-five years ago Nick Clawson donned his first Santa Suit. It was ten years ago, however, just after his sixty-fifth birthday, that his salt and pepper hair had turned thoroughly white, his beard had become sufficiently full, and his belly, never slim, but certainly never fat, had grown splendidly robust, giving him the distinction of the perfect department store Santa Claus.

It was a distinction Nick always wore proudly, although with his many years of hearty service about to come to a close it was one he now wore sadly.

It all started a few years back… in his knees… arthritis. It had been one thing to get out of bed in the middle of the night just to go to the bathroom, but walking all day long during the holiday season? That had turned into quite another – especially with the jaws of winter biting at him every step of the way.

Unfortunately the arthritis soon moved into Nick's shoulders, neck and back, the spasms and swelling so severe at times he couldn't straighten up or turn his head; and then one day while Nick was outside shoveling the snow from his walk, his chest tightened. For a moment, one that seemed both brief and never-ending, he stood hunched over, trying desperately to calm his trembling body. It was of no use, however, and Nick finally dropped to his knees, where he remained in silent prayer to Jesus until the sweat on his forehead dried and his staggered breathing returned to normal.

"Why not move to Florida?" They all asked him after the incident? "Why hang around here just because you get to play Santa Claus one month a year? Hell, you can do it down there, can't you?"

"Yes, but I like it here," Nick would respond graciously. "Besides, Christmas is supposed to be celebrated in the winter, in the snow. At least that's the way my Santa Claus sees it."

"Your Santa Claus? What the hell does that mean, your Santa Claus?"

"It just means that's the way I feel inside, that's all," Nick would respond with a faint smile and a gentlemanly tip of his hat.

And so it was that Nick continued living in Polar Town. Eleven months a year he stayed inside his tidy two bedroom house, reading books, watching old movies and living comfortably off of his pension and social security. But come the day after Thanksgiving and Nick would be dressed in his Santa Suit and out the door by seven o'clock in the morning. For the most part, he'd spend each day exactly the same way too. Early morning was reserved for greeting kids outside the elementary school with big hugs and booming, Ho-Ho-Ho's! Mid-morning to early afternoon was spent ringing his Christmas bell and collecting money for the Salvation Army in the small downtown district where he was usually good for twenty dollars a day. Then it was time for lunch, although Nick never ate. Instead he'd spend the next couple of hours visiting with kids in the children's ward at the local hospital – often times bringing gifts purchased with his own money.

Of course, the finest part of Nick's day would begin when he would arrive at Murphy's Department Store, where, after having two donuts and one cup of hot chocolate, he took his place in the sparkling Yuletide display, where kids would line up to sit on his lap and recite their Christmas wish-lists for the next several hours.

When Nick Clawson first volunteered his time to be Santa Claus he entertained a dozen, maybe fifteen kids a day, tops. He certainly never envisioned lines that were often one hundred kids deep. For that matter he never envisioned his popularity growing such, that children came from neighboring towns just to see him. Nevertheless, Nick would not cut short anyone's visit, usually spending ten absorbed minutes with a child. As such, when the department store closed for the night, there generally remained a fair amount of disappointed children. Still, it was his endearing manner that brought them out in the first place, so the disappointment was measured and most times dissipated completely with a pat on the head and a nice warm Santa smile, something each child was assured of before Nick left for the evening. Besides, they could always come back the next day, or even the next. In fact, those that did were commonly rewarded with an extra few minutes of Santa's time.

In all the years parents brought their children to see him, however, there were three who showed up once a week, for four straight weeks, several years in a row. They were Nick's favorites, for they provided him with friendship and sincerity even after they had outgrown the seat of his lap, because they still returned on occasion to say hello and to see how he was getting along.

And now, as Nick Clawson sat in his Santa Claus chair for the very last time, he looked at the large crowd of people who had come to thank him for the many wonderful years and noticed the three of them together. Each one holding a shopping bag full of gifts, they stood off to the side, smiling, though their misty eyes revealed sadness. Nick returned their smiles and after motioning them over, he did his best to hide the sadness in his own misty eyes.

Lucy Minnifield was five-years-old the first time she stood in line, clutching her mother's hand as though unsure if she was about to meet a nice fuzzy ol' grandfather type or Attila The Hun. But once she climbed aboard, her short legs barely dangling over Nick's lap, her trepidation vanished, and she smiled, and said, "Hi, my name's Lucy Minnifield."

"Hi Lucy, I'm Santa Claus," Nick replied, but instead of bellowing, "Ho-Ho-Ho," he gave her a nice big hug and whispered his standard greeting instead.

"I know who you are silly."

"You do?"

"Uh-huh, you're the man that brings presents to little kids like me."

"I am?"

"Uh-huh. I tell you what I want and then Rudolph drives you over to my house so you can give it to me."

"He does?"

"Uh-huh, but only if I'm a good little girl."

"I see," Nick said, gently rocking Lucy in his lap.

"But I am, so it's okay."

"So then, you listen to your mommy and daddy, right?"

"Uh-huh."

"And you eat all your vegetables, right?"

Lucy pondered her answer for a couple of seconds, before replying, "Uh-uh."

"You don't?"

"Uh-uh."

"Why Lucy Minnifield, which vegetables don't you eat?"

"Spinach... it's mushy. And I hate those green little ball things too."

"You mean Brussels sprouts?" Nick asked, with a smile as bright and cheery as the decorated Christmas tree behind him.

"Uh-huh, yeah, Brussels sprouts."

"Ho-Ho-Ho! So does Santa, Lucy. So does Santa. Ho-ho-ho!"

And every year from that one forward, Nick would ask, "Do you still hate spinach and Brussels sprouts?"

And every year Lucy would respond the same way. "Yep, uh-huh."

Even now, as Lucy approached Nick at the glowing age of forty-years-old, the first words out of her mouth were, "Yep, I still hate 'em."

Nick laughed, and said, "So do I, sweet-pea. So do I," his velvety tone somewhat obscured by an advancing sore throat.

"It's been a long time since you've called me that," Lucy said, the furrow of her brow caught in the melancholy of her own remark.

"Too long, I dare say, sweet-pea, too long."

Lucy took hold of Nick's hands, and then leaned over and warmly kissed his cheek. "Do you remember the first time you called me that?"

"What, sweet-pea? Of course... you were ten years old. You came to see me thinking you were too big for my lap. But you weren't, were you?" Nick asked mindfully, his long white hair skipping across the tops of his shoulders as he shook his head. "You were having problems with that girl at school. Martha, I believe she called herself."

"Martha Burbidge," Lucy said.

"Yes, that's right, Martha Burbidge. She was busy telling everyone how ugly you were. *Don't play with Lucy at recess*, she ran around saying, *or you'll be ugly too. Don't sit next to her in class, or you'll look just like she does. Don't walk home with her from school, or you'll be too ugly to have any friends.*" Nick winked. "Of course, the topper was when she said that you were too ugly for Christmas. That not even Santa Claus would bring you a present."

"But he did, didn't he?" Lucy asked, her big brown eyes smiling with affection. "In fact, Santa Claus showed up at my school everyday for the next week to bring me presents and walk me home. And you made sure that everybody saw us. Especially Martha Burbidge."

80

"Yes, well…"

"Well nothing," Lucy said. "It was the single nicest thing anyone has ever done for me. Right up until the time you did something even nicer. Something I've never forgotten. Something I'll never forget."

Nick responded with a look of uncertainty.

"The mirror. Don't you remember… the magic mirror?"

"You mean the one with the painted glass border? You still have it?"

Lucy reached into her bag. "Look familiar?" She asked, as she held it up.

Nick smiled. "Yes, I guess it does."

"Remember what you told me… that a mirror is something people use to see how they look on the outside. But that this mirror is magical because it lets people see how they look on the inside, where the real beauty is. All I had to do, you said, was look in it everyday and as soon as I accepted what I saw, I could never be ugly, and never feel lost. It was a little over my head at the time, but I did what you told me anyway. I looked in it everyday, until one day it all made sense. And every last drop of it is true. I'm just sorry and ashamed I haven't told you how important that was to me until now." Lucy kneeled beside Nick's Santa Claus chair. "It changed my life," she whispered. "You changed my life."

"I didn't change anything, sweet-pea. You did. You're the only one that could have. All I did was provide you the seeds to grow a little confidence. It's as simple as that."

Lucy gazed at Nick for several thoughtful moments before reaching into her bag again. "I've got a present for you," she declared. "But you can't open it until Christmas day, alright?"

"A present, for me? But why?"

"Yes, a present for you. And because."

"Well that hardly makes any sense."

"Actually you dear soul, it makes perfect sense. If anything, it's much too little, much too late."

"Hey, who's the Santa Claus here, me or you?" Nick asked, without taking notice of the neatly wrapped package she put in his lap.

Lucy bit her bottom lip and stood. "You are. You're the real thing," she replied quietly. "Absolutely the real thing."

Seconds later Nick watched as Lucy Minnifield walked away in wistful silence, the lump in his throat quelling all but a "Thank you" when she turned and waved goodbye one last time.

Buddy Kincaid sported long dark curls, deep green eyes, and a smile that could light up a room even when he had yet to make his way past the entrance. But when he tried to speak, he had great difficulty, as Nick discovered the first time they met, a little over thirty years ago.

"What's your name, son?" Nick asked, motioning Buddy to walk over.

Buddy dug his hands in his pockets as he approached, slowly, cautiously, but it wasn't until he was situated on Nick's Santa Claus lap and Nick asked his name a second time that he stuttered, "B' B' B' Buddy, K' K' Kin', Buddy Kincaid."

"Well now, it's a real nice pleasure to meet you Buddy Kincaid. I'm Santa Claus. But I bet you already know that, don't you? Bet you know that I live in the North Pole and that Rudolph is the reindeer with the shiny red nose too?"

Buddy quietly fidgeted in his seat.

"You know what I bet you don't know, though?" Nick asked, with a boyhood twinkle in his eyes. "That Mrs. Claus, my wife, is a yucky cook. She tries hard but most nights I have to send Rudolph out to pickup a pizza and some ice cream for desert. That's how I got this nice big tummy of mine," Nick declared, rubbing his belly. "So, what about you Buddy... you like pizza and ice cream?"

Buddy nodded.

"What's your favorite flavor? Strawberry, chocolate... or is it," Nick suggested, while moving his bushy white Santa Claus eyebrows up and down, "tutti-frutti?"

Buddy grinned, but as Nick continued to twist his expression to-and-fro, he started to chuckle, stopping only after Nick's face settled back into its Santa Claus roundness, and he said, "You look like a chocolate man. Am I right?"

"Uh-huh, I like ch' ch' ch'..."

"Chocolate," Nick calmly interjected.

"Uh-huh, ch' ch' chocolate," Buddy calmly repeated.

Nick patted Buddy on the back. "So what's on your Christmas list this year? A new bike, maybe?"

"I umm, I umm, I already ha' ha' have one."

"Maybe a racecar set then, huh? Or better yet, a train set. Wait... wait, I know – how about a brand new itchy sweater?" Nick asked, prodding Buddy with a gentle poke in the ribs before swallowing him up in a big Santa Claus hug.

Buddy wiggled free laughing. "You're f' f' f' funny."

"I guess that means you don't want the itchy sweater then, huh?" Nick asked, watching in delighted silence as Buddy laughed once more.

"Uh-uh," Buddy finally replied, his long dark curls dancing back and forth as he shook his head.

"Uh-uh?"

"Uh-uh."

"Okay, no itchy sweater, but I'll bet you're looking forward to Christmas anyhow, aren't you? Big family dinner – loads of presents – school vacation. Favorite holiday, maybe? What do you say Buddy, yea or neigh?"

"Yea."

"It's my favorite holiday too. But I have different reasons. Want to know what they are?" Nick asked, tilting Buddy to the side so that he could get a better view of him.

"O-k' k' kay,"

"Because every year, I get to meet somebody really special. And this year that somebody is you."

"It is?" Buddy asked, his nose scrunched up in curiosity.

"Sure is. And ya know why my little friend?" Nick asked, his tone ringing with animated splendor. "Because you remind me of me when I was a lad your age. Oh, don't get me wrong. You're the handsome devil I never was. Probably quite the little ballplayer too. But you're quiet, just like I was quiet. It's almost a scared kind of quiet... know what I mean? Like you're afraid nobody wants to hear you talk."

Buddy scanned the line of kids waiting for Santa, but otherwise remained silent.

Nick angled closer and whispered, "You think your stuttering gets in the way of the things you want to say, so you say nothing at all. You think everyone is too busy to stand around until you can get the words out... or that maybe they'll make fun of you while you're trying to get the words out. Is that it? I mean, I know that's how it was with me. Is that how it is with you?"

Buddy confronted Nick's earnest Santa Claus expression for a few moments, before saying, "I'm sc' sc' scared t' t' to t' t' talk. I'm scared to talk."

"Yes I'm sure you are, but you know what's interesting Buddy? You just did the very thing you said you're scared to do. You talked. Perfectly, I might add. It just took you one try before you could say everything you wanted to. And I think that's pretty great."

"You d' d' do?"

"Yes, I really do. You know what else I think, though? I think you can do even better."

"You d' d' do?"

"Absolutely son. Absolutely."

"B' B' But how?"

Nick shrugged his Santa Claus shoulders. "I'm not sure it's safe to tell you. I mean, I want to and everything. I'm just afraid you might laugh at me."

Buddy shook his head emphatically. "N' N' No, I w' w' won't."

"Promise?" Nick asked sheepishly.

"P' P' Promise."

"Okay, and if I promise I won't do anything to hurt you, will you also promise to do what I say?"

"P' P' Promise."

"Good, then I want you to close your eyes and count to twenty to yourself. And while you're counting I want you to try and picture the numbers in your head. Can you do that for me?"

"Uh-huh."

"Are you sure?" Nick asked, moving his bushy white Santa Claus eyebrows up and down again.

"Uh-huh," Buddy replied smiling.

"Alright, then I want you to begin right now."

Buddy sealed his eyes but after a few moments Nick asked, "Are you picturing the numbers in your head as you count them?"

Buddy nodded.

"You sure you're not thinking of the way I make my eyebrows do the herky-jerky?"

Smiling from ear to ear, Buddy nodded once more.

And every year from that one forward, Nick would ask, "Can you still see the numbers?"

And every year Buddy would respond the same way – with a smile from ear to ear.

Even now, as Buddy approached Nick, his dark curls still long, his presence still very striking, he offered Nick a gregarious smile, and said, "I still see 'em."

"Yes, but it's obviously no longer necessary," Nick stated with a gleam in his eye.

"Thanks, to you," Buddy replied, and then leaned over and kissed Nick's Santa Claus cheek. "It's nice to see you. I'm sorry it's been so long."

"You don't need to apologize for being busy. You're supposed to be busy, aren't you?"

Buddy lowered himself to one-knee. "I wouldn't be busy if it hadn't been for you."

Nick patted Buddy on the shoulder. "Nonsense, even though it's nice of you to say."

"It's not nonsense, and you know it. In fact, if you hadn't asked me to come back to see you after that first day, I'd probably be sitting in a corner, stuttering to myself right now."

"No, you would have found another way."

"Maybe… I don't know," Buddy said rolling his eyes and head simultaneously. "What I do know is that you gave me an abacus, which I still have by the way, and my life began to change from that day on. Do you remember?"

"What, the abacus? Sure I do."

"Not the abacus, the day itself."

"Of course. You showed up like I asked and I gave you a couple of pointers on how to use it."

"No, no, no," Buddy said, shaking his finger. "You're not getting away with any of that."

"Any of what?" Nick asked, the mirth in his soft eyes waning.

"Any of this, *I didn't do anything special routine.* You didn't just give me a couple of pointers. You taught me how it could help me with my speech. Remember? One bead represents one syllable. One syllable represents one complete sound. Use it everyday, you said. Read books and move the beads accordingly. Practice until the beads match the syllables and the syllables match the completed sounds. Then practice until I can visualize the beads as syllables and the syllables as words, because once I can visualize my words, you said, I would be able to say them properly. Remember?"

"Visualizing words is an old Chinese proverb. I just took it a step further, that's all."

"Oh, so you know all about Chinese proverbs, eh?" Buddy quipped.

Nick winked. "I deliver toys to China, remember?"

"You know what? You probably do," Buddy replied, his words clinging to the waft of laughter that flew from his nostrils. "In fact, I hope you do because that'll mean some little kid is probably going to benefit greatly."

"Well if it hasn't happened by now it's probably not going to because after today I'm hanging up my sleigh."

"I know, and speaking of which, I got you a little retirement present. A Christmas gift, really."

Nick held up his Santa Clause hand as though a stop sign. "You know that's unnecessary. I only did for you what you would have done for me if the situation were reversed. It's really that simple."

Buddy retrieved the package from his shopping bag and placed it next to Nick's Santa Claus chair. "I don't think the situation could ever be reversed because I could never be you."

"Sure you could."

"No sir, I couldn't. I don't have the bounty of your spirit."

"Listen, Buddy," Nick began, before having to momentarily stop to clear the catch in his throat, "a little self confidence and a lot of hard work go a long way. Now I may have helped you to believe in yourself, but you and all your hard work took it the rest of the way."

Buddy stood up and kissed Nick's Santa Claus forehead. "I don't know where you're from, or what's inside you, but you're surrounded by a whole lot of magic."

Nick dropped his gaze to the floor and after swallowing hard, looked up, and uttered, "Thank you."

Buddy squeezed Nick's Santa Claus arm and said, "No... thank you."

Ridley Preston was born without two toes on her left foot. It made walking painful, limping noticeable and teasing by the kids at school, inevitable. It was also the very reason she had a hard time looking into Nick's Santa Claus eyes when she first sat on his lap, some thirty-plus years ago.

"What's the matter child?" Nick asked, struck instantly by a demeanor so young, and yet, so apparently lost among the ruins of timidity and fear.

Ridley looked up, looked away, and then promptly shrugged her shoulders.

"Come now, you can tell me. I'm Santa Claus. You don't have to be shy or afraid around me."

Ridley kept her eyes glued to the floor, although once Nick started to stroke the back of her head, the comforting gentleness of his touch seeping through his glove covered hand, her apprehension began to recede, until finally, she looked into his inviting Santa Claus eyes. "I don't have all my toes. And everybody laughs at me at school and calls me gimp."

"I see... and what do your mommy and daddy say about it?" Nick asked, while stealing a quick peek in the direction of where he thought Ridley's mother might be sitting.

"They tell me to quit being a baby."

Nick wrapped his arms around Ridley. "Well, you know what they say about people who tease other people, don't you? They say they tease because it helps them feel better about themselves. Do you understand?"

Ridley sank deeper into Nick's warm Santa Claus embrace. "You smell just like peppermints."

"Peppermints? Well are they at least scrumptious peppermints?" Nick asked, the size of his festive grin hidden beneath the overflowing whiteness of his mustache and beard.

"Of course they are silly. And I think I kinda, sorta understand, too."

"Kinda, sorta?

"Yep. Kinda, sorta."

"Well then, perhaps this ol' peppermint smelling Santa can kinda, sorta explain it like this," Nick said to the delightful giggle of Ridley Preston. "Sometimes people, kids and grownups alike, are missing something inside their bodies. Just like you're missing toes, they're missing a feeling of some kind. No one knows what the feeling is exactly, but if you could look inside their bellies you'd see a big empty hole right where this feeling is supposed to be. And just like you can't grow yourself new toes, they can't fill this hole."

"So what do they do?"

"They use your feelings to fill it."

Ridley turned to face Nick. "They do? But why?" She asked, the youthful clarity in her brown eyes a stark contrast to her puzzled expression.

"Because that's the only way they can ever feel whole, or feel good about themselves. Unfortunately, all it really does is hurt you."

"What do you mean, Santa?"

"Well child," Nick began with a long Santa Claus sigh, "in order for them to feel pretty, they have to make you feel ugly. In order for them to feel nice, they have to make you feel mean. In order for them to feel strong, they have to make you feel weak. In order for them to feel good about themselves, they have to make you feel…?"

"Bad," Ridley exclaimed on cue.

"Exactly, they have to make you feel bad. And in your case that's why they tease you. It helps them feel good and strong. So… do you understand it any better now?" Nick asked.

"Kinda, sorta," Ridley replied, her fluffy blonde hair bouncing across her face as she briskly nodded her head.

"Kinda, sorta, huh?"

"Yep. Kinda, sorta."

"Ya know, there's a good part to all of this," Nick suggested, just as Ridley fell back against him.

"There is?" She asked, springing forward.

"Yes. You can help your problem. They can't help theirs," Nick replied.

"I can? But how?"

"By becoming a dancing angel, child. By becoming a dancing angel."

And every year from that one forward, Nick would ask, "Are you still a dancing angel?"

And every year Ridley would respond the same way. "Do you still smell like peppermints?"

Even now, as Ridley strolled toward Nick, her childhood limp – just that, the first words out of her mouth were, "Do you still smell like peppermints?"

"I don't know, are you still a dancing angel?" Nick returned, his laughter, though not as hearty as in years past, all the invitation Ridley needed to fill his outstretched arms.

"I'm just as angelic as ever," Ridley teased.

"Yes, but do you still have the shoes?"

"The magic shoes? Are you kidding?" Ridley asked as she drew back from Nick's Santa Claus embrace. "I have them hanging on my wall. They're encased in Plexiglas."

"Plexiglas... why?" Nick asked, the deep wrinkles across his forehead and around his eyes making him look old, however serene.

"Because they're the most important possession in my life. They have been from the moment you gave them to me." Ridley offered Nick a sardonic grin. "Do you even remember that day?"

"Child, I may be old, I'm not, however, without faculties. Not only do I remember that day, I remember the baffled look on your face when I first showed them to you."

Ridley sat down at the foot of Nick's Santa Claus chair. "But they were so strange looking."

"Yes, I know. I had to convince you they were actually shoes before you would even put them on."

"It wasn't so much that as it was convincing me they would help me walk," Ridley said, pulling at the wavy ends of her hair.

"Ahhh, but that's the thing, child. They didn't help you walk. They allowed you to dance. They gave you the opportunity to learn ballet and to become a ballerina. But... but," Nick added while wagging his glove-covered finger back and forth, "it was only after practicing day in and day out – strengthening your feet, building power in your legs, discovering the muscles of balance, and, most importantly, ignoring all the pain, that you were able to help yourself walk normal."

Ridley took hold of Nick's hand and brought it to her cheek. "Say what you want, the shoes were magical. And you, you dear sweet soul, you were magical for giving them to me. You changed my life in ways I can never express."

Nick flashed a discerning smile. "I did nothing but give you the confidence you needed to try something that might help. But it was you, child, who did the work. Not I... never I."

"I disagree," Ridley replied, as she led Nick's hand back to the arm of the chair. "Because once I was able to walk normally, I stopped being afraid of people – stopped wondering who was going to tease me next – stopped wondering who was going to push me from behind to see if I'd fall – stopped wondering if I was really different from everybody else. And you knew it would happen. But then, you see things no one else does. Don't you?"

Nick smiled again. "Child, I just see what's in front of my face. That's not special. It just means I take the time to look, that's all."

Ridley's gaze dropped to the floor, where, after a thoughtful pause, she peered into the sunset of Nick's Santa Claus eyes, only to feel her own eyes tear up. "I have something for you, but I'm like Lucy... I don't want you to open it until Christmas day, okay?" Ridley pulled a small, gift-wrapped box from her bag and put it in Nick's Santa Claus lap. "I love you," she said, as she stood to kiss his cheek. "I really do."

Nick wanted to say, 'I love you too,' but his quivering jaw would only allow him to mouth the words. So he did.

It was almost ten o'clock in the evening before Nick Clawson entered the front door of his house on North Street. He was cold, having walked the last half-mile against a surly winter wind, and certainly hungry, having had very little to eat since the crack of dawn. And yet, like a peaceful shadow cast from the weightlessness of a full moon's light, or the silent flicker of a star, far, far away, he felt at ease.

The house, as usual, was empty, and except for the sound of his boots crashing together as he cleaned them of snow, the occasional grunt or sigh that slipped out when he took off his Santa-suit, or the wood floor creaking beneath him as he moved about, it was silent as well.

But just as it had always been empty, it had always been silent. There had never been a wife, or kids. There had never been any sisters or brothers, Nick having been an only child, born and raised into a lonely family where his mother was routinely despondent and his father routinely absent. There was once a cat, however. A Persian beauty named Prancer. Unfortunately, Prancer died long ago, breaking Nick's heart and returning him to the barren landscape of his life, where he has since remained, without companionship.

Nick dragged his slipper-clad feet across the cold linoleum kitchen floor, and after fixing himself a snack, he headed for the family room. It was small room, but it was also his favorite room in the house. It had two cushy chairs with a matching couch, a coffee table, a moderately sized color TV, a fireplace that didn't get used but once a year (on Christmas Eve), and in the corner, a small Christmas tree decorated with a single strand of peppermint sticks (the scrumptious kind, of course). The tree was so small, in fact, there was barely enough room to fit his gifts underneath.

Still, it was a problem Nick Clawson cherished, for it was the first time in his life that he had received a Christmas gift from anyone, let alone three different gifts from three different people. Yet, there they were, as real as real could be. Which one would he open first, Nick wondered? Perhaps the gift he received from Lucy. It had the prettiest wrapping paper. Red and green with silvery white snowflakes, it stood out like a snowman in spring. Then again, Buddy's gift was the biggest... and definitely the heaviest. Yet, there was Ridley's to consider. Hers may have been the smallest, but it had a homemade ribbon tied across it and Nick found that particularly thoughtful and loving. Fortunately, Christmas was a day away so there was still plenty of time to decide.

Nick finished his snack and then stretched out on the couch where his gaze landed on the photographs hanging from the wall. Cheery faces inside cheery frames, some were old, some were new, but every single one of them was taken during his Santa Claus years.

And as he studied the faces of his oh-so-many-children, his tokens, his mementos, he located pictures of Lucy, Buddy and Ridley and he was reminded of the gifts waiting for him underneath his Christmas tree.

Yet, when Christmas morning arrived, the gifts remained unopened, for on Christmas Eve, Nick fell into the embrace of heaven's sleep.

Long Journey's the Angel

Long sleep's the white dove
Under crescent moon
The midnight pearl

Long rides at daybreak
The chestnut mare
A Cherokee girl

Long flow's the river
Ageless drifter
Of time and space

Long journey's the angel
Oh crimson god
Amazing grace

Long stand's the mountain
Imposing guard
Stalwart king

Long grows' the bounty
Fruited plains
Eternal spring

Long shine's the starlight
Eyes of night
Mystical face

Long journey's the angel
Oh crimson god
Amazing grace

Long stretches' the highway
Patches of glory
Trails of sin

Long craves' the restless
Utopian need
Beggar-man's skin

Long fall's the mighty
Wayward bound
Homeless disgrace

Long journey's the angel
Oh crimson god
Amazing grace

Long cry's the heartache
Sullen eyes
Wounded soul

Long keep's the memories
Seeds of life
Life made whole

Long walk's the hero
Solitary man
Solitary pace

Long journey's the angel
Oh crimson god
Amazing grace

Long chill's the winter
Barren touch
Frigid glare

Long bloom's the flower
Rainbow skies
Sunny stare

Long drift's the shadows
Seasons of change
Leather to lace

Long journey's the angel
Oh crimson god
Amazing grace

Long play's the music
Liberty bell
Silent night

Long spin's the dancer
Ballerina child
Essence of light

Long bleeds' the lonely
Crowded life
Empty embrace

Long journey's the angel
Oh crimson god
Amazing grace

Long sleep's the buried soldier
Flowers of wood
Gardens of stone

Long searches' the fatherless child
Castles of sand
Marrowless bone

Long dream's the unborn baby
Broken promise
Hollowed face

Long journey's the angel
Oh crimson god
Amazing grace

Long hide's the dark side
Easy smile
Raging twin

Long lives' the madness
Hated neighbor
The color of skin

Long thunder's the heavens
Darkness, darkness
Endless space

Long journey's the angel
Oh crimson god
Amazing grace

A Special Place
1970

Daisy Jo Starr arrived at Mansfield General Hospital within an hour of her first contraction. Two days later she was still there, drifting between the seemingly endless pain of giving birth and the hopeless despair of having no place to go, or no one to turn to once she was released. It was, to be sure, the very reason Dr. Lewen chose not to disturb her, instead patiently waiting for Daisy to pull her eyes away from the window and look at him. Though when she did, she surprised him with a faint, yet heartfelt smile.

For someone the nurses labeled a callous, condescending man, Dr. Jack Lewen was anything but; maybe a little rough around the edges, but not nearly as bad as the nurses portrayed him to be behind his back, and never, ever at the expense of his patients – especially Daisy Jo. When it came to her the good Doctor went out of his way to be as gentle and caring as any Doctor possibly could. Although, given that Daisy's home life disintegrated long ago, her two best friends, Cora and Laney, were living the lives of college freshman over two thousand miles away, and the father to be was nowhere to be found when it mattered most, gentle and caring were relative concepts.

Still, Dr. Lewen was all the gentle and caring Daisy had, so when he cradled her hand between his own and asked how she was feeling, the question floating out of his mouth with the delicacy of a leaf floating in an autumn breeze, she welcomed the opportunity to bury the stormy uncertainty of her tomorrow under the calming affect of his presence, if only for a moment's eternity.

"Better, thank you."

"Ya know," Dr. Lewen added, with a wink of an eye, "I wouldn't ask if you weren't my favorite patient. And just in case you don't believe me..." Dr. Lewen stepped away from the bed, and after pantomiming his way through a, *'nothing up my sleeve routine,'* pulled a fudgsicle from his coat pocket and exclaimed, "voila`!"

Daisy did her best to play along, although her best consisted of an impassive, "Bravo."

Dr. Lewen fashioned himself an exasperated pose. "Do I detect a bit of the humdrum? Could it be you think little of my magic? Because if that's the case, my dear Daisy Jo, let me assure you, this was no ordinary feat, because this…" Dr. Lewen displayed the fudgsicle as if the entire world were looking on… "this is no ordinary fudgsicle. No siree Bob. This one is magical. Magical because it disappeared from the private little stash Nurse Gurney keeps for herself in the nurse's lounge." Dr. Lewen peeled off the wrapper and offered it to his patient. "Actually I could have hunted one up in the cafeteria, but it's a lot more fun when I steal them from Gurney. Upsets her somethin' fierce. Especially when it's her last one. The ol' tyrant's gonna have a cow."

Daisy was in about as much mood to laugh as she was to eat, but when Nurse Gurney unexpectedly bellowed, "So this ol' tyrant's gonna have a cow, eh Dr. Lewen," startling the Doctor such, he threw his arms in the air and sent the fudgsicle sailing in the process, she couldn't help herself. Either could Dr. Lewen, who, after turning around to discover the fudgsicle landed within inches of Nurse Gurney's overstuffed size nine shoes, unleashed a bellyful of laughter better suited for a man twice his size. Still, he managed to choke it back long enough to retrieve the fudgsicle and stick it in Nurse Gurney's hand, whereupon he promptly closed the door, leaving the fuming nurse to fume on the other side, while he, of course, filled the room with another bellyful.

Unfortunately, Daisy didn't share the Doctor's enduring appetite for laughter.

And as long as she continued to be plagued by the image of her father, a man who nine months earlier wailed away at her damnable pregnancy with a fervor equal to one of his Sunday morning fire and brimstone sermons, she, in turn, a curled up, battered and beaten mess on the cold and muddy ground before him, laughter wasn't something she could easily manufacture, let alone sustain. No sir. With the destination of each day sewn from the fabric of a haunting past, Daisy's moments of laughter were but a sputtering few.

And just like now, even then they were often a prelude to tears.

2

Martin Starr, Reverend Martin Starr, dismissed the notion of the bald tires and icy roads having something to do with the accident as just plain silly. He wasn't swayed by the empty flask found in his wife's purse or the smell of whiskey found on her clothes either. "She was a poor driver Officer Mathews. It's the good Lord's way of remindin' the rest of us that poor drivers got no business bein' on the road. That's why the car hit the tree, and that's why she died. Nothin' else to it."

At some point Officer Mathews pretty much expected to hear God brought into the mix. But even at that, he never expected to see such a pathetic display of emotion coming from a Reverend. "Downright cold," he would explain to his wife, Betty Sue, later that evening. "And then when that cute little Daisy gal burst into the room, the Reverend looked at her like she'd just done somethin' bad, and said, with me standin' right there, mind you – 'You're mama was in a car wreck. She's dead. Funeral will be day after tomorrow. Now go to your room and let me n' Officer Mathews here finish up our little talk.' Fred Mathews shook his head in disbelief for what must have been the umpteenth time that day. "I'll tell ya Betty, I never saw nothin' like it. That young gal just stood there with her eyes waterin' and chin quiverin' somethin' awful, and all her daddy could say was go to your room. Dang it all, she can't be no more n' eight years old. Kinda makes ya wonder what the hell's in store for her." Fred Mathews shook his head one last time before plopping down in his easy chair to watch TV.

Betty Sue Mathews wasn't very fond of the Reverend herself – hadn't been ever since she overheard him call Carl Taylor a no good lazy nigger all because he asked the Reverend if the church could spare some clothes for his mama and sister. Nevertheless, having recently read an article in Life Magazine about how death can affect loved ones in a variety of ways, she wasn't altogether convinced Reverend Starr's reaction wasn't simply a matter of that. Convincing her husband – now that would take some doing. Not because he wasn't the convincing type, because she wasn't a real quick thinker, let alone a quick talker. As a result, by the time she figured out how best to explain the article, 'I Love Lucy' was already blaring away on the television. And once that happened about all she could hope for was an obligatory nod of the head.

What Betty Sue didn't realize, however, was that her husband saw Reverend Starr's face, and with it, a pair of deeply set, brooding eyes that couldn't have penetrated his daughter Daisy with any greater a chill than if they'd been carved out of ice. It was a look even Lucy Ricardo couldn't shake loose – one that would have elicited the same less than pacifying response regardless of what Betty Sue hoped to explain. It was a look Fred Mathews would carry around for a long, long time.

3

Martin Starr, Reverend Martin Starr, leaned his sturdy back against the wall and took a quick pull from the whiskey bottle. There was a time, five, maybe six years ago, when he'd take a sip from a bottle and all hell would break loose on his insides. First his eyelids would flutter like two wings flapping in the wind, and then his throat would tighten up, as if protruding veins would somehow block the whiskey from making its way down to his stomach, where finally it would land, crashing like a fireball and sending him into a momentary tailspin. But it wasn't that way anymore. Now the Reverend barely winced, and more often than not it wasn't from the whiskey at all, but rather the anger he was trying to soothe by drinking it in the first place. Sometimes it worked – sometimes not. Either way, when Sarah was alive she never noticed much shift in her husband's behavior.

Sarah Littlefield was twenty years old the first time she laid eyes on Martin Starr. She went into a grocery store to find some peaches so her mama could make a peach cobbler for desert that night, but instead found Martin standing in the aisle filling a bag with apples. With wavy jet-black hair and a profile that revealed sleek features and perfectly smooth skin, she found him to be quite handsome too. But when he suddenly looked up and caught her gawking at him, his dark, engaging eyes an instant reminder of the picture she kept on her nightstand of Tyrone Power, awkwardness took hold, stranding her with the notion that any attempt at conversation would only make her sound like a clumsy fool. It seemed a much easier task to simply look the other way... so she did... (albeit slowly).

Martin, on the other hand, couldn't remember the last time a girl took note of him that way – especially one so pretty. And since he couldn't recall the faces of any other pretty girls still living in town, he guessed her to be a newcomer. 'Course, it could be that her and her mama came down from Mount Gilead or some other neighboring town because the shopping was better in Mansfield. Not that it really mattered. What mattered was the twinkle her bright green eyes couldn't hide each time she glanced over her shoulder at him. Warm, inviting, and as far as Martin was concerned, the sign from God he'd been waiting for, for oh so long. The slender gal with the fresh face and strawberry blonde hair, the stranger who just happened into the grocery store at the precise moment he was filling a bag with apples all because he woke up that same morning with a peculiar hankering for fruit (peculiar because he wasn't very fond of fruit and couldn't remember the last time he actually ate any), was obviously no coincidence at all, but the woman meant to bear his son. It was for that very reason Martin approached her. "If they sold flowers here I'd surely grab a handful for ya. But since they don't, how 'bout an apple instead?"

Sarah giggled. Yet, having been somewhat comforted by the ease in his deep voice, she wasn't feeling quite as bashful as she might have sounded. "I bet you offer flowers to all the girls in town. Don't ya?"

Martin shook his head. "I grew up around here. Most of the pretty girls I knew either moved away or got married. Sometimes both. No one left I'd be interested in pickin' 'em for anyway."

"Oh, go on," Sarah gushed, with a wave of her hand. "Handsome fella like you doesn't have somebody special? I don't believe it. Not even for a second."

Martin kicked at the floor as a touch of red filled his face. "C'mon now, you're makin' fun of me, aren't ya?"

"Not at all. In fact," Sarah was quick to add, "I think what you said about the flowers was real sweet."

"Well, I don't know if it was sweet or not. I just know the good Lord wanted me to say something before ya walked away so he stuck the words in my mouth to make sure I did."

Sarah bit her bottom lip.

"Didn't say nothin' wrong, did I?"

"No," Sarah replied, as the sparkling green in her eyes softened under a reflective gaze. "Truth is, for a second there you sounded just like my granddaddy. I mean, except for him, I never heard anybody say the good Lord was the reason certain words got spoke. And now you. I guess it just took me by surprise, is all."

"Well now I'm truly sorry. Last thing I wanna do is surprise you like that. Heck, it's bad enough I got a bellyful of butterflies. No sense you havin' 'em too."

"Don't fret. Anytime I can think about my granddaddy is okay by me."

"Must be a special sort of fella."

"He is. Probably 'cuz he's been my grandfather and daddy all in one."

Martin's good sense told him her real daddy must have passed away. He asked anyway.

Sarah sighed. "Nah, he's alive. At least we think so. Haven't seen him since I was a little girl though. Used to be he was livin' somewhere around Chillicothe – workin' in the patch as a tool pusher on a drilling rig. Granddaddy figures he still is. Anyway, a long time back my mama grew real tired of all the excuses he used for never comin' home. So did my granddaddy. I mean it was his son and all, but granddaddy didn't think that gave him the right to stay out drinkin' and foolin' with other woman all the time – especially on Sundays. If nothin' else, granddaddy always expected his son to come around for Sunday church and supper. But it wasn't too long before he stopped comin' around even then, and I think that made granddaddy maddest of all." Sarah shrugged. "I guess since he was the Reverend over at the church in Bucyrus, him bein' mad about it only stands to reason though. Don't you think?"

Martin could have nodded his head a dozen times, but it was the hint of youthful innocence in his otherwise reticent smile that captured Sarah's attention.

"What? What'd I say?" She asked, the spirited tone in her voice kicking up a hint of her own youthful innocence. "Or was I was talkin' too fast. Mama and granddaddy always tell me I'm talkin' too fast. I don't think so myself, though I guess it's possible."

"No, you weren't talkin' too fast. And yes indeed, I think your granddaddy had reason to be upset. Your daddy wasn't respectin' the fact that the good Lord created Sundays for church worship and family gatherings."

"Careful now," Sarah cautioned in jest. "You don't wanna sound too much like a Reverend unless you're entertainin' the notion of becoming one. And just so ya know, my granddaddy says it ain't a responsibility befittin' just anyone."

"Well now, I appreciate the warning. But seein' as how I lead the congregation at The Church of Christ right here in Mansfield, I think it's a little late." Martin set his bag of apples on the fruit stand and offered his hand. "I'm Reverend Martin Starr. I'd be real pleased if you'd call me Martin, though."

"Well Martin, I don't know if anyone's ever told ya, but you look too young to be a Reverend," Sarah replied, the flush of embarrassment warming her face as she offered her hand in return. "Just the same, my name's Sarah Littlefield. I live over in Bucyrus."

With a regal dip of his head, Martin said, "Well Sarah Littlefield, I'm thirty-one years old and happy to make your acquaintance."

Sarah played along and curtsied as best she knew how. "The pleasure is mine Martin Starr. The pleasure is mine."

4

Looking back on it Russell Littlefield couldn't remember the last time he enjoyed a Sunday dinner more. It wasn't just the food (although being able to keep down the chicken fried steak and sweet corn was a definite bonus), for once the conversation wasn't glued to his poor health, stupid town gossip, or the latest in women's fashions. Best of all, he was able to enjoy a little after supper sipping whiskey without having to worry about getting chastised for it by his granddaughter, Sarah. It wasn't that Russell was a big drinker and couldn't wait to latch on to a bottle of bourbon, mind you. Russell simply believed a man was entitled to an occasional drink without having to first attend someone's funeral. "It's like this," he explained to Sarah the last time she caught him spitting up a mixture of blood and phlegm all because of the rot gut he sampled the night before, "iffin the good Lord created whiskey solely for the purpose of lauding the dear departed then there wouldn't have been much need for prohibition, now would there?"

Sarah didn't know any more about prohibition than she did the creation of whiskey, but was willing to bet that her granddaddy didn't either. Still, she had no more interest in exploring his opinion back then as she did in disrupting what had been a perfectly good Sunday simply by scolding him about the whiskey he was drinking now. For that, Russell had Martin Starr to thank.

Martin arrived at the Littlefield residence at precisely half past four. Though much of the morning and early afternoon had been a promising mix of sun and clouds (more promise than anything else), by the time Martin pulled up to the white frame, two story farmhouse, the face of the distant yellow sun was shining high above, surrounded by a world of shimmering blue. It was the perfect setting for a porch swing and glass of lemonade. And when Martin reached the front door, Sarah offered him both.

Russell was tinkering around with an old tractor engine out back and didn't hear Martin pull up. He had to stop every so often, however, to cough up the mix of blood and phlegm Sarah had become all too familiar with over the past year. Good thing she ain't lookin' at the stains on my hanky right now, Russell thought. Otherwise she'd see more blood than spit and figure the sickness has gotten worse.

And then I wouldn't be eatin' chicken fried steak for supper no matter who she invited over. She'd boil something that would likely taste poorly and make me eat that instead. Good ol' Martin Starr. Ain't met him yet, but he's already done a heap of good for my diet. Too bad it took Sarah two months to bring him by. Now, if I can just keep the coughin' to myself, I may even get away with a glass or two of whiskey after supper. Russell snickered while making his way over to his favorite tree stump for a little rest.

No sooner did he sit down to relax his lungs, however, when his daughter-in-law, Charlotte, called out to him from the kitchen window. "Sarah's company is here. They're sittin' on the front porch. Now go wash up and introduce yourself. You can rest later."

Russell didn't have to look up to know Charlotte was casting a watchful eye over him. Every time he moved, it seemed, day or night, indoors or out, she studied him. And if he should be bold enough to ask what in God's name she was looking at, Charlotte would huff, puff and blow out the same answer every time. "Nothing. Believe me, you're not all that soft on the eyes to look at. I'm just makin' sure you're still movin'. You'll have plenty of time to rest when ya die. Till then, stay off your ass. Lord knows it's the only time you get any exercise."

Truth is, when it came to her father-in-law Charlotte was a lot like Sarah. She flat out worshipped the very ground he walked on. If it hadn't been for him, there's no telling where she might have ended up… let alone how, or with whom. Sadly enough, the closer she sensed Russell's death, the more she sensed her own failing health. Nevertheless, Charlotte refused to let on. She couldn't afford to, what with the future of Sarah's family life still uncertain and all.

"Did you hear what I said old man? Sarah's company is here. Now take your lazy ass and go wash up so you can introduce yourself like a gentleman. Who knows? Ya might just fool him."

Russell would have liked nothing more than to ignore his daughter-in-law, but since he wasn't of a mind to deal with the nagging that would have surely followed, he calmly picked himself up from the tree stump and headed for the screen door, though not without getting his two cents in first. "Listen woman, if the good Lord didn't want me to rest whenever I felt like it then he wouldn't have struck this ol' tree with lightning so I'd have a place to sit down. The way I see it, the only problem with this tree is that you weren't sittin' in it when it got struck."

Charlotte turned away from the window and covered her mouth for fear Russell would hear her laugh.

During all the years he spent as Reverend of The Church of The Almighty, Russell Littlefield bent over backwards to render himself a clean and learned man of God. At a minimum, that included polished shoes, crisp white shirts, and a wit, both fit and proper. It also included well-manicured fingernails – although since Reverend Littlefield liked to work in his garden when he wasn't tending to church business, well-manicured fingernails weren't always easy to come by. Nevertheless, Russell tried scrubbing them two, sometimes three times a day. Then his illness took hold and Russell felt obligated to retire from the church – retiring, as well, the notion that polished shoes and crisp white shirts were a necessity of daily dress. As for his fingernails, well, let's just say since Russell gave up trying to clean them for the good Lord himself, he had no intentions of cleaning them for Sarah's beau, fellow Reverend, or not. Of course Russell still washed his hands, and the moment he pushed open the screen door and walked on to the front porch, he extended one, along with an inviting smile. "I heard a rumor we had a visitor out here. But I can see it's no rumor at all."

Martin couldn't get up from the porch swing fast enough, leaving Sarah to scurry for the middle just to keep the swing balanced. "Reverend Littlefield, Martin Starr. Reverend Starr actually. It's a pleasure to meet you."

Martin's grip was firm, almost too firm, given Russell's age and weakening condition. Suffice it to say he was somewhat relieved when Martin let go. "No need to have stood up son. And please, call me Russell. My Reverend Littlefield days are days gone by."

"What do ya mean? You'll always be Reverend Littlefield," Martin protested. "Heck, if the good Lord intended for it to be any other way, people wouldn't still refer to you that way. And I know for a fact they do 'cuz I had to stop for directions on my way over. One mention of your name and it was Reverend Littlefield this, Reverend Littlefield that."

"Well now son," Russell said as he rubbed his day-old beard, "if you're gonna look at things by way of the good Lord then by golly I 'spose you're right. On the other hand, if the good Lord wanted people to fly, he wouldn't wait till they were angels to give 'em wings, now would he?" Russell glanced at Sarah and winked. "Of course, if someone had mentioned that to the Japanese beforehand, we might not have had to deal with Pearl Harbor."

Martin didn't have to say he was confused – the cockeyed look on his face did the talking for him.

Russell blew a stream of air from his nose and snickered. "I'm just foolin' with ya son. Go on now, have a seat. I need to ask you somethin' serious." Russell waited for Martin to sit down and then promptly leaned forward, his blue gray eyes jumping with far more life than his body had left, and asked, "How do ya make a tissue dance?"

Martin responded with a blank stare.

"C'mon now son. How do ya make a tissue, you know a hanky, a tissue, how do ya make it dance?"

Martin shrugged his shoulders and said, "Gee, I plum don't know."

"Ya put a little boogie in it. Get it? Ya put a little boogie in it."

Martin stole a quick peek at Sarah, and then looked back at Russell Littlefield before cutting loose with a handful of strained laughter.

"Pretty good one, ain't it? But I got better. For instance, whataya get when ya cross one of them little weenie dogs with a mouse?"

"I forgot to warn ya," Sarah broke in giggling, "but granddaddy thinks he should've been a comedian. Don't worry though, he's the only one who thinks so, so ya won't have to keep humorin' him."

Martin folded his arms and leaned back in the swing. "Heck, I gotta good laugh from it. Matter-a-fact, your granddaddy oughta think about takin' his act on the road. One day a Reverend funny man, the next day... who knows?"

Russell threw his hands on his hips. "Who knows, you say? Who knows? Well my friend let me be the first to tell ya. My comedic talents are just a scratch at the surface son. Just a scratch at the surface. Shoot a bird, you oughta catch some of my other talents," he said, and then launched into a little song and dance routine. "I oughta be in pictures...I oughta be a star...I oughta be in pictures...I oughta be a star...da da da da da da...da da da..."

"What's goin' on out there?" Charlotte called out. "Russell, you actin' up again?"

Russell stopped, although it was his growing apprehension over a coughing attack, not because of anything Charlotte had said. Russell merely blamed it on her, that's all. "Nothin's goin' on out here. Now just mind your P's and Q's woman and leave the entertainin' to me." Russell took a couple of long, wheezy breaths, leaned close enough for Martin to be able to count the beads of perspiration on his forehead, and in a half whisper, said, "I'll let you in on a little secret, but you gotta promise me ya won't say nothin' to Sarah's mama. Okay? Is it a deal?"

Martin nodded, reluctantly.

Russell cared not. He was going to have some fun with or without Martin Starr. "The fool woman's always stoppin' me right when I'm gettin' warmed up. And ya know why? She's jealous of my talents. Always gonna be too. Especially my singin' and dancin'. Now Sarah here, she's more jealous of my joke tellin' abilities. Not that it really matters. What matters is they both know I could make it in Hollywood and they couldn't. Ain't that right Sarah?"

Sarah rolled her eyes.

"C'mon now Sarah, forget all your face makin' and tell this fine young Reverend of a lad that you and your mama know I could make it."

Sarah thrust the back of her wrist to her forehead like the great actress she wasn't, and sighed. "Yes Martin, I'm afraid it's true."

"Ya see that!" Russell blurted out. "What'd I tell ya. "I'm a man of vastly talents bein' held back by people with none at all."

"Yep," Sarah added, "as long as he took his truck and remembered to gas up along the way, Russell could make it to Hollywood all right."

Martin almost did a double take. "You call your granddaddy by his first name?"

"Relax silly, it ain't nothin'," Sarah replied, her long strawberry blonde hair the perfect compliment to her effervescent smile. "Besides, I only do it when he's actin up… like now."

Martin was getting a cockeyed look on his face again so Russell decided to do what he could to add to it. "Hell son, iffin ya think that's somethin', you oughta hear the names her mama calls me. I think it might be sinful just spelling them. Can't wait to hear what she calls you."

"Oh pay him no mind, Martin. He's just carryin' on. Probably tryin' to scare you off is all."

Russell snickered.

Martin quickly sipped his lemonade, and then said, "Heck, I ain't goin' nowhere."

5

True to his word, Martin Starr, Reverend Martin Starr, didn't go anywhere. On the contrary, in the six months following his first visit for Sunday dinner, he was on his way to becoming as permanent a fixture at the Littlefield home as that old tractor engine Russell liked to tinker around with out back.

Though much stayed the same during that period, including Martin Starr, Reverend Martin Starr, a few things had indeed changed. The sun no longer bathed under a canopy of sparkling blue. Instead, it spent most days hiding behind ugly winter clouds. The wind no longer danced from morning till night like a butterfly floating in a gentle summer breeze. Rather, it ripped across the open flats and attacked with the treachery of a pack of hungry wolves. And Russell Littlefield no longer did a comedy routine in the middle of the afternoon, or sat on his favorite tree stump wondering how long before Sarah got on him for sipping whiskey after supper. The cancer in his body wouldn't allow it.

For Sarah, it was a time when months disintegrated into weeks, weeks disappeared like seconds, and standing vigil at her granddaddy's bedside day after day was to witness the childlike twinkle in his eyes succumb to the swift, yet methodical ravages of pain. A time when dreams were no longer real, prayers went unanswered, and Sarah screamed her anger at the distant, pale moon as though it was the face of the good Lord himself. It was a time when Charlotte offered as much as her own deteriorating state would permit, Martin offered as much as he deemed appropriate (which generally consisted of doing the few odd chores Russell used to do), and loneliness, dreaded loneliness, reared up its ugly head and offered everything it could. A time when Sarah, a young woman whose granddaddy always said was as bright and cheery as the daisies he once planted in his garden, was slowly becoming a hollow replica of that very description.

Unfortunately it would all become much worse, for on the morning of Sarah's twenty-first birthday, just days after Russell was laid to rest, her mama collapsed from heart failure, and it was then, the beginning of a profound and never-ending sadness.

Prior to her mother's passing, Sarah couldn't recall a single instance when she used her good china. Oh sure, there were times when Charlotte took it out for the occasional dusting, but only because she wanted the china to look its sparkling best whenever she showed Sarah what would one day be her wedding gift, same as it was Charlotte's when she got married. But there had been no wedding for her mother to attend, only a funeral, and Sarah, nevertheless, found herself washing an assortment of those very same fancy plates and cups all because Martin thought it the only proper way to serve cake and coffee to a house full of people. "If Doc Wilson and the rest of your neighbor friends are of a mind to come out in this foul weather so they can pay their respects to your mama and wish you a happy birthday at the same time then it's only fittin'," he declared. "Lord knows them plates won't give a hoot. No reason you should."

Another time and Sarah would have likely expressed a far different opinion on the matter. As it was, however, she said nothing, wanting only to cry herself to sleep and put an end to her grieving, if only for the brevity of a single night.

But sleep wasn't to be – not until the friends, neighbors and well-wishers who'd come to extend their sympathies were given a chance to do so, even though Sarah resigned herself to the kitchen and Martin resigned himself to accepting many such gestures on her behalf – not until all the cake and coffee disappeared and the small talk ran its course – not until Martin Starr, Reverend Martin Starr, had ample opportunity to lead the room in one final, booming prayer.

And even then, not until Sarah was alone in bed and Martin's parting words to her, "The Lord takes those from us only when he leaves the gift of another," took their resting place among the silent confines of a dark and empty house.

6

Martin Starr, Reverend Martin Starr, knew that Sarah was meant to be his wife and the mother of his sons from the moment he caught her gawking at him like a little schoolgirl with a runaway crush on her hands. The fact that he hadn't been privy to that kind of look in quite some time didn't change his belief one little bit. Heck, with her mama and granddaddy both passing away not more than a couple of months back, it was understandable. So too was the notion that she seemed as put off holding hands with him as she did sitting next to him on the porch swing; although with the weather still walking on shaky ground, the porch swing was an iffy proposition at best. No matter. Martin figured just as soon as he asked for her hand in marriage, Sarah would cut loose with one of those long lost, wide-eyed smiles of hers, dust off the past, and then jump up, and shout, "Yes! Yes! Yes!"

But Sarah didn't offer him a wide-eyed smile. Nor did she jump up and shout anything. She simply thought about the arduous task of living life without her mother and grandfather, bowed her head, and quietly sobbed.

"Dangnabbit," Martin hurled, as he folded his arms and tapped his foot to the beat of his racing pulse. "What in God's name are ya cryin' for now? I know me askin' you to marry me might've snuck up on ya some, but damn woman, it ain't cause to go off the deep end again. Christ Almighty, that's all ya seem to do these days."

Sarah lifted her head, her long hair serving as a tattered shield for her weary eyes and runny nose, but said nothing.

"C'mon Sarah, ain't ya got no words for me at all?"

Sarah dabbed her eyes with a half-soggy tissue, and then nodded. "You're right Martin, I haven't been very fair to you, will you forgive me?" She asked, her voice little more than a scratchy whisper.

Martin responded with a brisk head bob. "Apology accepted. Now, how 'bout it? How 'bout if Sarah Littlefield becomes Sarah Starr?"

Once again Sarah met Martin's question with silence. This time, however, Martin didn't plan on hearing a rousing, "You betcha," come flying out of her mouth. By the same token, he didn't plan on letting his marriage proposal die off so quickly either. With the passing of Sarah's mama and granddaddy leaving her a weak, guilt stricken wreck, Martin knew if he just kept pressing, getting what he wanted was only a matter of time. "Heck, Sarah, how many times in the past couple of months did ya tell me ya didn't do enough to please your mama and granddaddy when they were alive? Better yet, how many times did ya tell me ya feel like you were a failure and a disappointment to 'em? Heck, I even recall hearin' you say that if you had at least gotten married before your mama and granddaddy passed on, you could've eased some of their pain 'cuz they wouldn't have felt so bad about desertin' you. Well now, Sarah, we both know the good Lord's got 'em in heaven lookin' down on you right now. But what you haven't figured out is that if ya just say yes to me, they'll know about it and be real happy. Real happy indeed."

Sarah remained quiet, but as she gazed at her mother's china cabinet the solemn expression on her face crumbled under the weight of her mounting uncertainty and words were no longer necessary.

Martin walked over to the couch and promptly kneeled. He thought it only fitting to take hold of Sarah's hands, yet, when he realized she was still clutching the soggy tissue between them, he rested his fingers against her kneecap and squeezed it instead. "First time I ever saw you the good Lord whispered in my ear that you were meant to be my wife. I been waiting for ya ever since. Waitin' to make you a good husband. Waitin' so that we could get started on a family of our own. You'll see, Sarah. I'll take such good care of you, it won't be long till you're 'bout as happy as you've ever been. I promise you that. Lord knows I promise you that."

Sarah stared at Martin until the shallow creases around his engaging dark eyes deepened, hinting at the warmth of a smile. Only then did she break her silence, when she bowed her head and sobbed once more.

Sarah had no idea what to expect, but at the same time she didn't think it would hurt the way it did; certainly not enough to make her yelp. Of course, it didn't help any that Martin jammed himself inside her, all the while grunting and drooling like a savage beast attacking its poor, unsuspecting prey. Luckily Sarah only had to wait a few minutes for Martin to finish, whereupon he abruptly collapsed on top of her, gasping until it no longer sounded as though each breath of air was certain to be his last. Then, just as abruptly, he rolled off, curling up with his own sweat while Sarah remained hopelessly still, left to embrace her loneliness and the obscure sounds and shadowy images that only a dark and unfamiliar setting can bring about.

Some six months passed since that first night, but along the way Sarah found herself getting used to living in Mansfield. She was even getting used to living in the house Martin purchased with the money she made from the sale of her granddaddy's place in Bucyrus, even though she could have lived without the curtains Martin put up in the bedroom. It was one thing, and bad enough at that, to have such an ugly mix of colors hanging in the room. But it was quite another when, because of the cheap fabric, the moon often peered through the window like a giant night light when she was trying to go to sleep, and the sun just as often screamed good morning with all the charm of an unexpected alarm clock when she was hoping to sleep in.

Still, Martin wouldn't hear of replacing them. "Those curtains are fine," he said with a curt wave of his hand, as if tossing Sarah's suggestion right out the window. "Heck, they're even better than fine 'cuz I picked 'em out. 'Sides, I know quality when I see it. You just ain't used to gettin' up so early, that's your problem Sarah. But don't fret, that'll soon change when you give birth to my son, who, by the way, I think I wanna name Christopher."

There were times, several in fact, when Sarah didn't share Martin's opinion. There were even a few occasions when she was a mere heartbeat away from saying as much. Nevertheless, there were only two instances when she actually did. The first occurred on their wedding night when Martin told Sarah it wouldn't be proper to celebrate their unity until they were living in their own house. "It'll be the purest way," he said, his arms folded tightly across his chest as though a show of support for his resolute tone. "It'll serve as a blessing to us and our house at the same time."

Sarah was a virgin, but nerves of a virgin aside, she also shared in the hope and curiosity of a healthy young woman. So much so, Martin's words proved to confuse more than stifle her. "That doesn't make sense Martin. Seems to me our marriage would be a blessing no matter what."

"It is. So?"

"So why did ya say what ya said?"

"Because I did!" Martin snapped.

"Well now, that ain't much of a reason Martin."

"Yeah? Well it is if I say it is Sarah, so ya best get used to it!"

"C'mon Martin, surely there's more to it than that. I mean what's a house got to do with…"

"Stop!" Martin suddenly roared. "Stop it right now!"

Sarah flinched, and then took a couple of steps backwards, not realizing she had moved, however, until the living room wall came out of nowhere to kiss her shoulder blades. "Whataya gettin' so mad about?" She asked sheepishly. "Just 'cuz I don't understand what you're getting at don't mean…"

"Damn-it Sarah, I said stop! Now stop!" Martin roared again, this time shaking his fist like he was banging a drum. "I don't expect you to understand nothin'! And I don't figure I have to explain nothin' to ya either! So just stand there, shut up, and be thankful when I do! You can do that much, can't you?" Martin moved a step closer to his wife and cocked his head. "Or ain't you no kind of woman at all?"

Sarah bit her bottom lip and looked everywhere but in the direction of her husband's rigid glare.

"There's somethin' you best realize Sarah. And the sooner you realize it the better off you'll be. I want my son conceived in the house where he's gonna grow up. Not your granddaddy's house, and not that back room in the church where I've been livin' these past couple of years. The house where he's gonna grow up. Where he's gonna live for a long time. Where he's gonna be nursed by you until he's old enough to learn how to be like his daddy. Only one problem Sarah, we ain't in that house yet. Won't be till I find us one. Until then, it's gonna be just like I said."

Sarah stood in silence, doing what she could to fight off the tears. For the most part she succeeded, surrendering only after Martin stormed out of the room.

The second time Sarah voiced her opinion actually occurred a few weeks later, when Martin suggested selling her granddaddy's house in Bucyrus with everything in it, which included the china Sarah's mother worked so hard to preserve. "Heck Sarah, if ya sell it all we won't have so much stuff to move. Plus, it'll mean more money for that house that came up for sale not spittin' distance from the church. Look at it this way, the furniture in here ain't nothin' special, it's just furniture. May not even match up with the new place. But there's a lot of it. More n' we'll likely need. So why not sell it and get us a few things that don't cost an arm and a leg. I don't know 'bout you, but I could sit on any ol' chair. As for those fancy plates and things you keep talkin' about, they're nice and everything, but fact is, they're just plates. Now the good Lord sees to it that people grow food, especially good ol' Americans. That's the important part, not what we use to eat it on."

Sarah picked up the serving bowl she just finished dusting and clutched it against her chest as if it were her favorite childhood stuffed animal. "I'm not selling my mama's good china," she replied, her jaw square, her conviction firm. "It's bad enough I'm sellin' this house. And I'm only doin' that 'cuz I know with you bein' a Reverend in Mansfield we gotta live there full-time. But that doesn't mean I gotta get rid of everything here. Fact is, after I let you sell my granddaddy's tools to Cleavis Bean, I decided that was it. I got some fine memories here Martin. Some fine keepsakes too. And the best one is my mama's good china. Now she wanted me to have it, so I intend to have it. I don't care what you say about it neither. That goes for the furniture too!"

Martin didn't really give a hoot about any damn china. He merely suggested its sale because he figured Sarah would concede to selling everything else as long as she was allowed to hang on to that. What Martin didn't figure on, however, was figuring wrong. He didn't like it either. Didn't like it one little bit. And when he unexpectedly bellowed, "You'll do as I say, when I say it," then wrestled the serving bowl away from Sarah and sent it crashing against the wall, he made it quite obvious too.

Sarah shrieked, and then dropped to her knees, crying frantically for every piece of the broken bowl worth picking up, and desperately for every piece that wasn't.

Still, that was many months ago, more than enough time for Sarah to come to her senses and realize that the first disagreement with Martin had as much to do with the stress of being newlyweds as the second one did with the stress of finding a new home. Now if Sarah voiced an opinion that was perhaps different than Martin's it would simply be that of a wife and expectant mother discussing a situation with a husband and expectant father. Certainly nothing to think twice about, which is exactly why Sarah didn't. "You never mention me havin' a baby girl Martin. But there's just as good a chance for a little girl as there is a little boy. And if we have one, ya can't very well name her Christopher, now can you?" She asked with a twinkle in her eye and a cheerful smile on her face.

Martin stopped dead in his tracks, and without so much as turning around, uttered, "It'll be better for you if I pretend I didn't hear you say that. Now don't ever say any such thing again. Not ever."

It may have taken several moments for Sarah to respond, but with a look of unfettered disbelief gripping her on the outside, and a combination of pain and anger exploding on her insides, it was all Sarah could do just to gather up enough calm to take a seat at the end of the bed, much less say anything. And even when she did, she had to fight to keep her voice from cracking. "Say what Martin? I'm talkin' about us havin' a baby girl 'stead of a baby boy. What's wrong with that? It's still a baby for peat sakes."

Martin's chest slowly expanded as he turned around and walked over to his wife. "Didn't you hear what I said?" He asked, his eyes petulant, his posture looming, and his voice ominous. "Now I warned ya once. I ain't plannin' to warn ya again Sarah."

Sarah dipped her head and rested her eyes on the old wood floor. "I heard ya Martin. I just don't see why ya gotta make me feel bad just 'cuz I mention the possibility of us havin' a baby girl."

Martin immediately grabbed Sarah by the collar of her nightgown and yanked her up from the bed. "If I thought you were ever gonna have a baby girl then we woulda never got married. The good Lord intends for me to have a son and that's just what I aim to have! Do you understand me?" When Sarah didn't immediately respond Martin repeated his question, only this time he shook Sarah, as if doing so would somehow jar an answer loose. Unfortunately, all it did was cause Sarah to start crying, infuriating Martin all the more. "If you're gonna insist on cryin' woman then I'll give you somethin' to cry about!" Martin held Sarah at arms length and proceeded to slap her across the face until he no longer felt like slapping her, at which point he threw her back on the bed and stormed out of the bedroom.

Sarah wouldn't leave the house after that, not for another three and a half months to be exact… when she went into the hospital and gave birth to a healthy baby girl.

Martin Starr, Reverend Martin Starr, didn't mind getting up at the crack of dawn – not as long as Sarah had his poached eggs, crisp bacon and buttered toast waiting on the table for him. It didn't matter if Sarah was up half the night because there was a diaper to change, a bottle of milk to prepare, or a helpless mouth to feed. As far as Martin was concerned, Daisy was Sarah's daughter, and as a result, Sarah's headache.

Had Sarah given birth to a baby boy, yeah, sure, Martin would have seen his way clear to a late breakfast every now and then. Heck, he might have even expected it from time to time. But the fact is, Sarah didn't, and because she didn't, Martin didn't figure it was his duty to tolerate much of anything. Not untimely food, which he would occasionally cure by throwing, plate and all, at his wife – not a screaming little baby with a stupid name like Daisy, who, by the time she was four years old, Martin had yet to pick up – and certainly not Sarah, who, despite Martin's recurring threats and at times volatile, if not altogether abusive behavior, continued to nurture her daughter in the kind of selfless, loving way that Martin was often reminded of the way his own mother nurtured and coddled his pathetic little sister, while he, of course, received no such affection at all. Until one night, when mother and daughter slipped out the back door while Martin slept and his father was passed out drunk, never to return, leaving Martin to spend the rest of his childhood absorbing all the affection his father could beat into him.

Ironically, Martin never held his father responsible, only his mother and pathetic little sister. Perhaps because he was too young to understand his mother's dire need to run away, not realizing she was tired of the drunken rages, tired of the beatings, and more than anything else, tired of screaming and crying in frustration while her daughter suffered at the hands of her husband's sexual perversions. Then again, perhaps it was because his mother didn't take him along, not realizing that every time she looked at him she saw the face and mannerisms of the man she married, a man she so desperately hated and feared, a man she couldn't get away from fast enough. On the other hand, maybe it had nothing to do with what Martin realized or understood, and perhaps was nothing more than this: His mother and sister deserted him. His father did not.

Regardless of the reason, however, Martin no longer wrestled with the ghosts from his childhood, the years having dulled much of the ugliness he endured. He was, unfortunately, left in an ageless struggle with a venomous anger that filled him instead. In fact, every day he was exposed to Sarah and Daisy chasing each other through the house like a couple of playful kittens, huddled together whispering silly little mother and daughter secrets, or just sitting around giggling, he thought of the life Sarah single-handedly ruined for him because of the son she didn't, and obviously would never have; convinced that Sarah giving birth to a pathetic baby girl was not a flagrant aberration, but a lifelong destiny. It was then that his anger became harder and harder to control. So much so, by the time Daisy was eight years old, he no longer tried.

Instead, Martin would simply erupt.

Dr. Lewen handed Daisy a small box of Kleenex before he pulled a chair up next to the bed and sat down. "When was the first time? Do you remember?" He asked.

Daisy didn't. Of course like most people Daisy didn't remember a lot of the things she experienced as a child. The experiences were there, mind you. They were just deep inside. Like lost treasure, bountiful, but of no use so long as they remained buried. Worse yet, no matter how far back her memory took her, Daisy was certain it wouldn't be far enough, which is why she replied, "I'm not sure it even matters Doctor. Let's face it, my poor mother had a son-of-a-bitch for a husband, just like I have a son-of-a-bitch for a father. But he was her husband long before I remember him being my father... ya know?"

Dr. Lewen leaned back in the chair and massaged his forehead, the long, drawn out sigh a finishing touch to his obvious contemplation. "I'm sure you're right Daisy. I'm sure your mother suffered plenty, and for that, I'm sorry – truly, truly sorry. But I wanna know about you. You're the one here. You're the one suffering now. And you're the only one I can help. So please, let me try and help you. Okay?"

Daisy would have liked nothing more than to warm herself with Dr. Lewen's unbridled kindness, but the weight of her hardship, past, present, and flat out cold, didn't make it easy. And though she obliged him the trace of a smile, when she said, "Tell me how to separate the two, 'cuz I don't know how," the melancholy in her voice smothered the hospital room like the gray clouds smothered the sunlight outside.

Dr. Lewen briefly pondered Daisy's question, and then shrugged his shoulders and said, "I don't know. Maybe you can't. Maybe you're not supposed to. Maybe that's what growing up in hell does to people. But ya know what else? You didn't let it destroy you when you easily could have. Ya know why? Because you didn't let yourself become your father. You don't hate – you hope. And that's made all the difference." Dr. Lewen inched forward in his chair and took hold of Daisy's hand. "I think it also has something to do with why you decided to give your child up for adoption," he added, somewhat reticent in his concern that any conversation about Daisy's newborn baby would unleash more agony than it would in providing the comfort and support he intended. "Even though it meant sacrificing your own happiness, maybe your only happiness, deep down you knew it was the best way, the only way to give the baby any kind of hope. And no matter what else happens, no matter how many times you might question your decision, always remember what you did took a great deal of courage and a genuine capacity to love. Do you... do you understand what I'm saying to you?"

Daisy squeezed his hand in return, and it was clear she understood. Indeed, she understood.

What caught Dr. Lewen off guard, however, was that Daisy abruptly turned her attention to the desolate gray outside the hospital window, as though trying to conceal the shame and embarrassment of tearing up, and said, her voice soft, but clear, "The first time I remember is when I was eight years old. I remember because it was my birthday. My mother had just finished putting the frosting on the cake she baked for me. It was chocolate. My father hated chocolate. Hate's it to this day. But mom knew it was my favorite so she made it anyway. Frankly, I think part of her wanted to do it just to get under his skin a little bit." Daisy smiled at the thought of her mother, a woman who, despite being married to a man that stripped her of both her youth and beauty while she was alive, had enough gumption to stick it to the bastard on her own terms whenever she could. "Anyway, just as my mother was opening a box of candles he walked into the room. I'm sure he noticed the chocolate cake and all, but I don't really think that's what set him off. Actually, I don't think he ever needed a reason, just an excuse. And that day his excuse was either in the whiskey he'd been drinking, or he realized my mother poured out half the bottle when he wasn't home and added water to it. Not that it woulda mattered a whole lot. It was Sunday... after his church service. He always got drunk then. So if the whiskey happened to be half water, it just took him a little longer, that's all." Daisy shrugged her shoulders. "I dunno," she somberly offered. "Mom once told me that my father only drank on Sundays. I guess she figured I'd believe her 'cuz I was too young to know any better. At the time she was right. But looking back on it, I think she was really just trying to convince me 'cuz that made it easier for her to believe herself. Maybe that's all she ever wanted – ya know, somethin' to believe in. Either way, the joke was on her. It didn't matter if my father drank a lot, a little, or not at all. I mean, when you're already a son-of-a-bitch, getting drunk only makes you a drunk son-of-a-bitch. Don't you think so?"

Dr. Lewen nodded his head without hesitation, but otherwise said nothing, prompting Daisy to turn away from the window and look at him. "Don't you think so?" She asked again, her eyes, though painfully bloodshot from days of crying and a lack of sleep, still soft, still youthfully blue, and, as always, still in search of something more.

"Yes," Dr. Lewen said, nodding his head again. "Yes, I do."

Daisy helped herself to a long, lingering sigh before continuing. "Anyway, before my mother had a chance to light the candles, my father grabbed her by the back of the hair and pushed her face into the cake. He wouldn't let her up either. She's suffocating and the lousy bastard's laughing. Can you imagine seeing something like that? Can you?"

This time Dr. Lewen wasn't as quick to answer, taking a few moments to envision an indignity he could barely come to grips with, let alone draw a picture of. And when he did respond, he did so by bowing his head and shutting his eyes.

"Oh, but there's more Doctor," Daisy promised, her voice fading into the shadows of a murky past. "My father never stopped until he humiliated you – over, and over, and over again." Daisy waited for Dr. Lewen to look up and take hold of her hand, at which point she promptly turned her head and stared out the window again. "There's a lot more."

10

The last thing Martin Starr, Reverend Martin Starr, expected was his sniveling little eight-year-old daughter attacking him from behind. Sticking her mother's face in birthday cake certainly didn't justify it. Hell, nothin' justified it. Nothin' justified the way she was carryin' on neither, what with all the screamin' and cryin' she was directin' his way. Even if she hated him, it wasn't right. Almost as disrespectful as hitting him. Noisier, that's for sure. One thing about it though. It wasn't gonna last very long. He'd see to that in a real hurry. Heck, why shouldn't he? His daddy never tolerated any disrespect from him. No reason he should have to tolerate any from Daisy.

Not today!

Martin threw Sarah against the wall then quickly spun around while she crumpled to the floor like a wet dishrag.

Not tomorrow!

He grabbed Daisy by the collar of her brand new birthday dress, pulled her unwilling body over to the counter and stuck her face in the cake. "Hit me, will ya. Well I got news for you," he growled, his fingers digging into the back of her head to hold her facedown and steady, "do it again and I'll break your hands. Ya got that? I'll break your hands!" When Martin decided enough was enough he latched onto Daisy's ponytail and tossed her to the floor, where her battered and beleaguered mother crawled to her aid.

Not ever!

Martin hurled the remains of the cake, platter and all, against the wall, aimed his finger and menacing glare at his cowering wife and daughter, and snarled, "The good Lord might've given me you two 'cuz he wanted to test my strength and loyalty, but don't think for a minute that means I gotta put up with any of your sass and nonsense. Not ever! You got that? Not ever!"

Sarah and Daisy got it all right.

If Daisy woke up screaming from her urine soaked bed in the middle of the night because she was having one of her all too frequent nightmares, Martin would storm into her bedroom to prove it was no nightmare at all. If Daisy was quietly playing in her room and Martin decided she should be scrubbing the kitchen floor instead, he'd pick up one of her dolls, rip it apart limb by limb, and then smack his horrified daughter upside the head and suggest she thank the good Lord it wasn't her. If Daisy left food on her plate, clothes on her floor, talked too loud, or simply whispered too soft, Martin would often display his contempt with a backhand across the face or a leather strap across the backside.

With Sarah it wasn't much different. If she showed any sign of protest when Martin raised a hand to Daisy, he would bellow the proposition, "Spare the rod and spoil the child" – and then make damn sure to apply the proposition to her. If Sarah didn't leave his pants perfectly creased, his shirts properly starched, or his shoes buffed and polished, he would lock her in a closet until convinced it wouldn't happen again. If Sarah spent too much time in her flower garden, failed to show up for Sunday services with a bright enough smile, didn't oblige his drunk induced sexual urges, or simply didn't move as fast, or jump as high as he might have wanted, Martin would temper her blatant impertinence by hitting her a little harder... a little longer.

And as the days passed... slowly... arduously, and the vitality of their family life reflected the ghastly colors of a bleeding stain, the shadows of Martin's wrath loomed larger, the hate in Daisy's belly began to take shape, and the weight of Sarah's fear and despondency grew heavier; so much so, while Daisy was in school one day and Martin at church, she buckled under the merciless and callous pressure, only to seek refuge in a whiskey bottle, and her dreams for another life.

11

Sarah's granddaddy always told her there were two kinds of whiskey. The kind you sip and the kind you swig. "Sippin' whiskey," he would proffer with his usual shoot from the hip expertise, "is meant to be enjoyed after a fine meal or with a good cigar. 'Course, since your mama don't know how to cook a lick of food, and I ain't much for smokin', I never have any. Swiggin' whiskey, on the other hand, is the kinda whiskey ya gotta plan for. Best way to drink it is to shut your eyes and hunch up your shoulders 'cuz when it hits bottom it's likely to burn a hole right through your feet. That's why ya gotta be ready for it. Iffin ya ain't, it can fool ya somethin' fierce. And the good Lord didn't put whiskey on this earth to fool nobody. Not even the Indians. They just weren't ready for it, that's all."

Sarah closed her eyes and basked in the glorious company of her smiling grandfather. "Granddaddy," she pleaded in a half whisper, "tell me what to do. Please, tell me. I feel so alone. I don't know anymore. I try to know. Lord knows I try to know. But I don't. Please tell me." No sooner did the words leave Sarah's mouth when the tail of a wintry gust whistled its way through the partially opened kitchen window and tickled her spine. She shuddered for a moment before opening her eyes to the image of her granddaddy shuffling over to his favorite tree stump, where he promptly sat down, laughed the kind of belly shaking laugh only one of his own stupid jokes could produce, and then topped it off with a little whiskey himself.

Sarah dabbed at the water forming in her eyes. "Sippin' or swiggin' granddaddy? Which is it?" She asked softly.

Russell Littlefield looked up but said nothing in return. He simply hoisted his glass, grinned that one and only devilish grin of his, and rode out on the tail of the same wintry gust of wind from which he first appeared.

Sarah rushed over to the window and pressed her nose against it, scanning the outside as though convinced her granddaddy was really out there and would pop into view at any time. Of course he didn't. In the bowels of her mind Sarah knew it too. Nevertheless she stood motionless, soaking up the numbing vision of her granddaddy until winter's biting chill ultimately returned her to the pit in her stomach and the whiskey she aimed to fill it with. And since it was whiskey

Martin bought, Sarah did just like her granddaddy said. She shut her eyes, hunched up her shoulders and took a swig. Then another... and another... and another.

Over the past three years Sarah grew consumed with gathering up the means so she and Daisy could escape the brutalities of their home life once and for all. She had wanted to run away as far back as she could remember, but decided to stay put, figuring it was better to wait until Daisy started school. That way she could put her plans into action and not have to worry about Martin breathing down her neck because she'd still have enough free time to keep up with her household chores.

Sarah figured right too. Martin's greed for money was such, it took a backseat to nothing – not his unconscionable demands for a squeaky clean house – not even his twisted beliefs regarding life, liberty and the pursuit of self-expression through persecution. All Sarah had to do was feed him half the money she earned. Not really such a bad deal though. Not when you consider that she was stealing back every nickel, dime and quarter she could get her hands on. She even got away with the occasional dollar when Martin was too drunk to notice. Unfortunately, in three years she only managed to reclaim ninety-two dollars. More than enough for a couple of one way bus tickets to Kansas, where the hopes and dreams of Daisy and Sarah lie somewhere over the rainbow, but not enough to start the new life she so desperately craved and Daisy damn well deserved. As such, no matter how many quilts and sweaters she had to knit, fruits and vegetables she had to grow, or jars of jams and jellies she had to fill, as long as there was a paying customer Sarah was willing to suffer at the hands of Martin a little longer.

But then the whiskey started creeping into her head, and her plans changed.

12

Sarah thought about packing up some clothes but decided there wasn't much point in running away if the clothes she and Daisy brought along carried Martin's stench. No sense making a clean break with a foul odor. "No sense at all," Sarah said, toasting her proclamation with a swig of whiskey.

As much as Sarah may have wanted to, she couldn't very well take her mama's fine china either. No time to pack it all up, and besides, after picking Daisy up from school she was only driving as far as the bus station. As such, even if she filled the car with boxes of plates and bowls she couldn't very well bring them on a bus. But the silver plated flask her granddaddy left behind? The same one she was filling with whiskey in order to keep her confidence high and anxiety low — now that was the one keepsake she would take with her. "Too pretty to leave to Martin, that's for dang sure," Sarah said, once again toasting her proclamation with a shot of whiskey before capping off the flask to go gather up her savings.

Three hundred and seventeen dollars might have sounded like a lot of money, it even made Sarah's purse slightly heavy, what with all the coins she never turned into paper. But considering her and Daisy were going someplace they'd never been before — with no family, no friends, no place to call home, and only the clothes on their backs, drunk or not, Sarah realized they were going to have to scrimp every step of the way until work could be had. Still, leaving Martin in such a hurry was the right thing to do. The whiskey told her so.

The whiskey also told her that dumping Martin's car at the bus station was as fitting as fitting could be. "Maybe the good Lord'll grow ya some wings so ya can fly over there to pick it up. If he don't, find yourself a ride. Or better yet, just walk. After all," Sarah said, regurgitating the very sarcasm Martin fed her whenever she asked to use the car, "someone with your poor drivin' abilities shouldn't be drivin' such a beautiful machine."

The fact is the beautiful machine was nothing more than a big ol' dirty Buick looking every bit its seven years. Martin knew it too. Nevertheless, he wouldn't allow Sarah behind the wheel unless he was too hung over to run his own errands or she had one of her deliveries to make, and only then because he got half the money she collected. Otherwise Sarah's stints behind the wheel remained far too few to garner any kind of feel for driving, much less driving the treacherous winter roads leading to Daisy's school. But hey, as soon as Sarah felt the tingly warmth of a little more whiskey, she knew she'd get there safely. The whiskey told her so.

Unfortunately, the whiskey lied.

When Sarah took the cutoff at Route 4, the short cut she was hoping for turned out to be on a road replete with patches of black ice. It would have been one thing if the road wasn't shaped like a snake, but since it was, no sooner did she negotiate the car around one bend when another one appeared out of nowhere to take its place. Worse yet were the never-ending ravines and gullies, that in July lined the road with streams of flourishing trees and wild flowers, but in January bared the hazards of a frigid and rolling landscape. Then, of course, there was the ice itself. Veiled by the ever changing shadows of daylight, capable of lashing out with the fury of a cracking whip, it occasionally stretched from shoulder to shoulder, making it as unavoidable to hit as the ominous trees waiting for Sarah as she spun out of control.

13

"In case you were wonderin' Daisy girl, your mama was running away when she crashed into that tree. Runnin' away from you."

Daisy turned from the window to look at Dr. Lewen, her wistful expression a constant reminder of the anguish in her heart. "I was twelve the first time my father told me that. Made my body start shaking like I was havin' my own little earthquake. Didn't matter to him though. He just kept repeatin' it throughout the day; stopping every so often, mind you, to laugh. By the next morning I woke up with a rash from head to toe. Guess I was havin' a reaction because of what was going through my head at the time."

"And what was that Daisy?"

"That it wasn't true. That it couldn't be true. Thing was, I had no way of knowin' for sure because my father, wonderful man that he isn't, created a pretty good element of doubt. The whole thing kinda put my insides on a collision course."

"But you know the truth now, don't you?" Dr. Lewen asked, his gentle tone all but lost in the shadows of his own skepticism.

"Sure, now I do," Daisy replied with a poignant smile. "Unfortunately now doesn't help when you're twelve years old."

Dr. Lewen took off his glasses and massaged the bridge of his nose, nudging the creases in his forehead out from under his thinning, dark hair in the process. "Maybe I'm missing something, but ya know what strikes me as odd," he mused, "that given your father's track record he would wait four years after your mother died before saying something like that. Granted, it's an ugly thing to say no matter when, but somehow I can't envision him waiting four days to say it, let alone four years. Why do ya suppose he did?"

Daisy didn't answer. Rather, she turned and gazed at the slumbering winter gray outside the hospital window, all the while trying to ignore the clammy chill racing up and down her spine.

"Did I... I didn't mean..." Dr. Lewen scratched his head. "Obviously I said something that troubles you. Didn't I?" Dr. Lewen waited for an answer until convinced the only answer he was going to get was a handful of uncomfortable silence, at which point he got up from his chair and joined Daisy at the window. "See anything out there?" He asked, like a stranger looking to pass the time by making idle chitchat with another stranger.

"Nothing but space," Daisy muttered. "Flat, ugly space. But a lot of it."

"Never been out of Mansfield, huh?"

"Farthest I've been is Toledo," Daisy lamented. "I was running away, hoping to get to Detroit. Figured it was a big enough city to get lost in until I decided where else to go. At the time it didn't matter. The only important thing was to be out of Mansfield and away from my father."

"When was that?"

"Couple years ago. I had just turned sixteen. Didn't even have my drivers license a week when I stole my father's car. Sure enough the police picked me up. Got a helluva beating for it when I got home too. Didn't make me want to stop tryin' though. It only made me realize I needed to make enough money so I could leave on my own terms and not have to steal his car again. Funny thing is, after I came back a police officer from around here gave me some money. Name's Fred Mathews. He said something about finding it at the scene of my mother's car accident. Said he was savin' it for me till he thought I was old enough. Unfortunately, my father stole it from my dresser before I could put it to use." Daisy secured her long blonde hair behind her ears and looked at Dr. Lewen. "Even so, that's when it all fell into place. That's when I first realized my mother didn't run away from me. She ran away from him. She was on her way to pick me up from school when she had the accident. No other way to explain why she was carryin' all that money or was on that particular road." Daisy pondered the sobering memory, and then hung her head and sighed.

"You okay?" Dr. Lewen asked.

Daisy nodded.

"You sure? If not, we don't have to keep talking. We can always pick it up again later."

"Really Doctor, I'm okay."

Dismissing Daisy's affirmation as little more than a poor attempt to depict a stiff upper lip, Dr. Lewen said, "Yes, maybe so. But just the same I think you ought to lie down."

Daisy agreed, yet continued to languish in front of the hospital window. "As for my father waiting until I was twelve – he wanted me to hate my mother for running away. It's as simple as that. He thought it would make me automatically respond to him. Ya know, I'd do whatever he'd tell just so he wouldn't leave like she did."

"Okay, but why twelve? Why not eight, when your mother had the accident? Didn't he want you to respond to him then?"

Daisy shut her eyes and hung her head once more. "I started to look good to him when I turned twelve. That's when he wanted me to… you know…"

"What do you mean, look good?"

"I was twelve," Daisy whispered. "I was fucking twelve."

Martin Starr, Reverend Martin Starr, sucked down the last of the whiskey and tossed the empty bottle on the ugly yellow and green checked carpeting. "Say Daisy," he called out cheerfully. "You sure are a pretty young thing for only bein' – what are you, twelve now? Damn! Growin' up just like a woman, ain't ya?"

When Daisy failed to respond, Martin called out once more. "Didn't ya hear me Daisy girl? I said you're lookin' real pretty. Why don't you come out of the kitchen and let your daddy have a look at ya? My supper can wait."

It took a few seconds for Daisy to figure out what to do but she finally moved the skillet off the burner and poked her head out of the kitchen. "But you know how you hate overcooked meat and I'm just about finished with it," she said nervously.

"Don't you worry none about overcookin' my meat Daisy gal. I ain't gonna punish you for it. Heck my days of strikin' ya for doin' all those things the good Lord knows ya shouldn't are over with."

"Well I probably oughta finish cookin' it anyway... in case umm... in case you umm... you know... in case you change your mind." Daisy bit her bottom lip and promptly disappeared back into the kitchen.

"Well why on earth would I change my mind?" Martin called out again. "Heck, I wouldn't have told ya my supper can wait if I was plannin' to change my mind, now would I? Of course not. Your mama on the other hand? Now she would have changed her mind. Heck, look at how she changed it over you. One day she wanted you, the next day she's runnin' away from you. That's why I'm always tellin' you she couldn't have been very interested in your wellbeing. Not like me, that's for sure. And if you're thinkin' about makin' some noise over her bein' gone – don't. No one's gonna listen to ya anyway. Heck, it's been four years. Carryin' on about it now would be kinda foolish, don't you think? I know I do. Matter-a-fact, I think it's downright nonsense. Heck, all that whining and everything – it's just silly schoolgirl stuff anyhow; and from the looks of it," Martin added with a snicker, "you ain't no schoolgirl. No schoolgirl at all. You hear what I'm sayin' Daisy? Huh? Do ya hear?"

Martin quit babbling long enough to peel off his grungy socks and marvel at all the dirt underneath his toenails. "Heck, look at it this way… I ain't runnin' off nowhere. Heck no. I'm gonna stay her to protect ya just like I'm gonna stay here to love ya. Enough for both a mama and a daddy. So whataya say ya come on over here and let me prove it to ya. Lord knows, now that you're startin' to look like a grown woman you're probably startin' to feel like one. Damn if it ain't worth finding out. So whataya say, huh? Put that meat aside and come on over here so I can rub your back for ya. Let your daddy start lovin' and protectin' you the way your mama never could."

Martin leaned forward to pick at a couple of his toes, but with the whiskey swirling around in his head and the mounting, if not altogether peculiar fascination he had with his feet, a couple turned into ten and it wasn't until his stomach gave way to hunger pains twenty minutes later that he realized Daisy was still camped out in the kitchen. Yet, when he marched in to find out why, the only thing he found was his meat simmering in a skillet, overcooked as usual. Daisy was long gone.

Ran off. Damn fool's probably at Laney Johnson's house. If not, Cora James' for sure. Troublemakers, that's what they are. Troublemakers, the both of 'em. Always fillin' Daisy's head with silly notions about… well, about somethin' that's for sure. No matter though. I'll visit with her when she gets back, Martin concluded. Maybe even wait until she's tucked away in bed. Be nice and cozy that way. Heck, I paid for the bed. And the good Lord knows that when ya pay for somethin' ya got the right to use it. Until then? What the hell – I'll eat supper, overcooked meat and all, and drink a little more whiskey. Maybe a lot more. What's the worst thing that could happen? A bad hangover? So what. I'm gettin' tired of answerin' to that stinkin' ol' church anyway.

As far as Martin Starr was concerned Charlie Bridger couldn't have come along at a better time. For one thing, he offered Martin the opportunity to buy into his filling station, aptly named, 'Bridger's Filling Station,' just about the time the Reverend and his church were about to part ways. For another, he offered the use of his pole barn, which gave Martin the chance to continue leading services to those people still attracted to his energetic sermons despite the vicious rumors and innuendoes that chased him out of the church in the first place.

The biggest reason, however, was because Charlie Bridger was the best friend Martin never had – a man with an insatiable appetite for liquor, any kind of liquor – a man who still swore allegiance to Jeff Davis and the Confederacy – a man who enjoyed nothing more than to don his little white hood and recite passages from the good book. A man, it turns out, who would have slipped inside his own daughter's bed if he didn't find her so utterly repulsive. "It's like this," he explained to Martin over a bottle of cheap Kentucky bourbon one Sunday afternoon, "your Daisy's a good lookin' young gal, so I don't blame you one bit for wantin' to explore her womanly charms. But now, you take my Amy Lynn – between her droopy ears and saggy belly she looks like that mutt dog of mine, only the dog might be easier on the eyes. Smells better, that's for sure."

"C'mon," Martin said, snickering, "it can't be that bad."

"Damn, boy, you think I'm joshin'? Well lemme tell ya somethin' Martin my friend, her bad looks ain't the half of it. She's dumb too. So dumb, in fact, I gotta call her Amy Lynn, Amy Lynn, because half the time she don't catch her name the first time around. She just stands there like a retard with drool hanging from her mouth. I'm not exactly sure what the good Lord was intendin' for her, but brains and good looks sure as hell weren't part of the package. At least not so far as I can tell."

"Ya know," Martin offered like a seasoned vet, "sometimes dumb ain't so bad Charlie. Sometimes they get smart and the next thing ya know they're gettin' a might too big for their britches."

Charlie peeled the bottle of bourbon away from his lips, wiped his mouth with the back of his hand, and said, "Havin' a problem with Daisy, are ya?"

Martin took hold of the whiskey bottle and rested it between his outstretched legs. "I guess I always figured her to be like her mama, not really capable of bein' much of a problem, ya know? But lately she's been a lot different than Sarah ever was. Puttin' up a pretty good stink, if I do say so myself. I mean she's always been resistful, but once I punished her nice and proper like, she pretty much fell back in line where she belonged. That's why I always likened her to Sarah in the first place. Now, though, it seems like the more I try to discipline her, the bigger the stink I gotta put up with. Why just a couple of weeks ago she bit my arm so hard, she pulled flesh clean off. I obviously smacked her around pretty good for it, but afterwards I had to leave her be 'cuz all I could think about was tendin' to my arm."

Martin promptly sucked down the last of the firewater, and after a rousing, "Ahhhhgggg," tossed the bottle on the dirt floor and watched it roll to a stop. "And if that weren't enough," he contended with a backhanded slap at the air, "why just a couple of days ago I sneak into her room after she's supposed to be asleep, only she ain't there. Heck, it had to be after midnight too."

"Where do ya figure she run off to?"

"Don't really know Charlie. For awhile there I was thinkin' she went to her friends. But then the good Lord made it clear... if she did that, she'd likely have to explain why she was poundin' on their door so late at night, and I don't figure Daisy for the volunteerin' type." Martin smiled at his best friend. "Heck, Charlie, for all I know she could be hidin' out in this ol' pole barn of yours."

Charlie smiled back. "Well then, if that's the case maybe you oughta let me know the next time she runs off. I'll go look for her myself."

Martin threw his head back and let fly a knee slapping cackle.

Charlie stole a quick peek around the barn.

Daisy Jo stared at Dr. Lewen, and yet, it wasn't until he asked her a second time that she responded, though barely compromising the vacuous look on her face even then. "Most of the time I just hid underneath my bed. I'd slam the back door like I was runnin' off somewhere, wait for him to chase after me, then sneak back in through the front and run up to my room. And since he was either too drunk of too stupid to catch on, I was okay. Scared shitless, but okay. I'd stay there till morning, makin' sure I was up and out of the house before he got up; which wasn't all that hard because he was usually still passed out from the night before. It didn't become a problem until I got older and couldn't fit underneath my bed anymore."

"Why, what happened then?" Dr. Lewen asked, his voice struggling to find some middle ground between his curiosity and his contempt.

Daisy manufactured a bleak smile. "Then I ran like hell for real. What else?"

Jack Lewen managed a bleak smile of his own, but otherwise said nothing, humbled, instead, by the stupidity of his own question.

"I didn't always get away though," she added, oblivious to the Doctor's abrupt silence. "Even though he was drunk there were times when he'd catch me. I'd do my best to get away, but sometimes, sometimes…" Daisy hung her head and swallowed back the ugliness of her words until they once again rested in the pit of her stomach.

"Listen Daisy, if you'd rather not talk…"

"The good part," she quickly broke in, "was that he finally gave up. The bad part was that it took me getting pregnant to get him to."

"Is that why you umm, you know," Dr. Lewen suggested, the placid reflection in his soft brown eyes vanishing the moment his eyebrows burrowed in above the bridge of his nose. "Is that why you got pregnant?"

Daisy leaned her tired body against the wall and slowly shook her head. "It wasn't supposed to be like this," she muttered, as though trying to convince herself of that very thing. "It was just, I guess, I dunno, Tommy said he wanted to marry me. He said he would take care of me. That's why I didn't think it was a mistake. I guess, I dunno, I guess it turned out to be one though, didn't it?" Daisy waited for Dr. Lewen to say something – anything. Yet, when anything turned out to be a question regarding Tommy's whereabouts, Daisy found herself somberly staring out the hospital window, where the snow blowing aimlessly only minutes ago, now fell in steady streams.

"Where the hell ya think you're going – huh?" Big, strapping Luke McCall barked at his youngest boy, Hal. "I thought I told you to stay put?"

When sixteen year old Hal McCall fumbled around for an answer, first by twitching like a nervous jackrabbit every time he opened up his mouth, and then by settling down long enough to calmly spit out a response, only to second guess every word that came to mind, Big Luke pulled his towering frame up from the chair and said, "Well? You gonna answer me boy, or you gonna stand there like a goddamn idiot?"

Given the chance, Hal McCall would have disappeared from the house without uttering so much as a single syllable. Yet, when all he could see standing front and center was a man too rugged to be anything less than thoroughly intimidating, a man whose all too familiar growl had a way of turning Hal's spine to mush, disappearing from the house wasn't much of an option. Nor was answering his father still much of a chore. Answering him without stuttering, however, was. "I...I...I was, I wasn't going anywhere. I...I...I was just go...go...going to work on Tommy's car."

"I thought I told you not to drive your brother's car. I thought I told you..."

"Just work...just working on it. That...that...that...that's all I'm doin'."

Big Luke threw his hands on his hips and thrust his square jaw forward. "Damn-it boy! Don't you have better manners than to interrupt me when I'm talkin'? Ain't your mother taught you better than that? Christ Almighty, ya act just like a goddamn idiot sometimes."

"T'...T'...T'...Tommy told me it was okay."

"Tommy told you what was okay – interruptin' me, or acting just like a goddamn idiot?" Big Luke folded his tattoo-covered arms and waited on his son's reply until one too many seconds rolled by and he grew tired of waiting. "Jesus Christ," he spewed impatiently, "if ya can't spit out an answer then do somethin' else. Nod your goddamn head if ya have to. Or do ya have trouble doin' that too?"

"No s'...s'...sir, I don't. And th...th...that's not...that's not what I meant either."

Big Luke laughed in the face of his son's flimsy declaration, and replied, "Never mind what ya meant boy. What's that stickin' outta your pocket there?"

Hal nervously kicked at the floor. "Ta...Ta...Ta...Ta...Tommy. It's a letter from Ta...Ta...Tommy."

Big Luke's laughter came to an abrupt halt, as did the ease in his expression. He peered sharply out of one eye, arched his brow into a menacing stance high above the other eye, and proceeded to walk over to his son, where, standing man to boy, his shadow devoured everything his derisive tone did not. "What the hell are you talkin' about, a letter from Tommy? Lemme see that."

"Ta...Ta...Tommy...Tommy wrote it to me," Hal protested, with all the piss and vinegar of a wilting flower.

"Yeah, right!" Big Luke sneered, as he took hold of Hal's shirt collar and slowly reeled him in. "Now gimmee the damn letter."

When Hal's only reaction was to protect his face, plucking the envelope from his shirt pocket was almost too easy. Yet, once firmly in hand, Big Luke didn't move, paralyzed by the image that his beloved son, though tarnished by the time and space of a distant war, was, for the moment, a mere letter away. Still, it wasn't until Hal tried to free himself that Big Luke thought enough to shove him from his grasp and actually read the letter's contents.

"Dear Hal,

By the time you get this little brother I'll be in a place called Khe Sahn. I don't know much about it. Except if it's like everything else around here, it'll be pretty damn scary.

I know I haven't written you before now, but before now nothing seemed to matter much. It's bad here little brother. Nothing like you could ever imagine. I think about dying about every 5 minutes or so. Can't help it. Not when there's people dying all around this place. That's why I'm writing you now. I wanted to tell you a few things in case something happens and I don't get the chance.

Anyway, I'm sorry for not being much of a big brother. I'm sorry I always pushed you around and made fun of the way you talked. I'm sorry for all them stupid practical jokes I played and for always blaming everything on you. Especially when dad was around. I know he can be pretty hard on you, and I'm sorry if some of that is because of the things I might have done. It wasn't right, and I sure as hell wasn't setting much of an example for you to follow.

Don't know why I was always acting like a big tough guy, except that maybe I was just trying to be like dad. Can't say for sure. Only know that there ain't no such thing as a tough guy around here. Ask any of the fellas and they'll tell you the same thing. We're scared. Real scared. All we ever talk about is going home, seeing our familys, sleeping in our beds – you get the picture little brother. All the things you're lucky enough to still be doing.

I wish I was home right now. If I was, me and you could toss the football around. Or better yet, go riding in my car. I miss that old car of mine. Never thought I would, but I do. Put alot of work into her, you know? Now that I'm stuck in Nam it makes all that work kind of special to me. Makes the car pretty special too. I guess it makes alot of things kind of special. You know what else though? Since you always liked my car I want you to take care of her while I'm gone. I never told you this before but you're good with your hands. Real good. Better than me and dad put together. So feel free to work on her all you want. And take her out for a spin whenever you get the urge. And if the old man yells at you for it, tell him it's my car and I said it's okay. Tell him it's my way of trying to make up for lost time. O.K? O.K.

If you want, take my bedroom too. I always had the better room, but as long as I'm not there to use it myself, I'd be real happy knowing you were using it. Just tell mom I said to toss my stuff in the closet, and you and me will work it out when I get back. O.K? O.K.

I got to sign off now Hal, but before I do there's a favor I need to ask you. It's pretty important too. I need you to give Daisy Jo a message for me. I need you to tell her that I'm sorry I left without saying goodbye. Tell her I didn't ditch her. Tell her I didn't lie. Not one time. Tell her I really do care about her. I just left because, I don't know. I guess it was more of that tough guy stuff. Tell her that's how I thought I was supposed to act. But tell her after being around here I found out that I ain't no tough guy. Tell her I ran off because all I really was was scared. I just acted to tough to admit it. Even to myself. Does that make sense little brother? I hope so. I hope she'll understand.

141

Tell her I think about her a lot. Tell her I love her.

Thanks little brother, and take real good care of yourself. And don't join up no war. No matter how tough you think you are, or how much the old man tries to convince you that joining up will make it tough. It won't. It can't. Do something smart. Go to college.

And Hal, don't forget me in your prayers.

Love,

Tommy

P.S. Tell mom and dad the next letter will be for them. If they get mad, just tell them I been writing them ever since I left home and hadn't wrote you one single time.

P.P.S. The next letter will be for you too."

"Ten days after Tommy's brother gave me that message, he brought me another one. Tommy's platoon was lost somewhere in the Khe Sahn Valley. He's missing in action." Daisy Jo paced herself with a deep breath, and in the process, eased the strain in her voice. "I was six months pregnant when I got the news."

The first time Dr. Lewen ever felt the nerves in his spine dig in, such that his body shuddered and his legs gave way, was the moment he learned of his wife's miscarriage. Rachel Lewen actually suffered two miscarriages, yet, since doctors deemed her chances for a successful pregnancy as extremely unlikely after her initial misfortune, Dr. Lewen wasn't as physically overwhelmed the second time around. By and large, his body simply filled with the basic pangs of anxiety; and though he never knew if they stemmed more from guilt, sorrow, or anger, he knew that every time he embraced the shadows of Daisy's ever deepening plight, he stood the risk of embracing the shadows of those same disconcerting feelings... over... and over... and over again.

Yet, when Daisy Jo unexpectedly quipped, "I wonder if I'd have the same rotten luck playin' poker as I do in life," Dr. Lewen was instantly reminded why it was a risk worth taking. And after tossing a handful of his own nervous laughter into the mix, he settled back in his chair, and said, "There's something I've been meaning to talk to you about Daisy. Actually, Rachel and I both wanted to talk to you, but now seems to be right, so I'll just have to do the talking for both of us."

"What's that?" Daisy asked, her anxious smile, though a portrait of pain and uncertainty, offering a glimpse at the enduring sparkle in her eyes nevertheless.

"Well, Daisy, basically it comes down to this," Dr. Lewen proffered, his comforting tone as inviting as any words he could ever hope to choose. "You're gonna need some time, quiet time, real time, to get back on your feet when you get out of here. And, so, Rachel and I got to talking about it, and, well, we'd really like it if you moved in with us."

Dr. Lewen quickly held up his hand to ward off whatever interruption might spring from Daisy's mouth. "Now the way I see it, you've worked on and off at Rachel's clothing store long enough for it to be perfectly obvious to anyone with a pair of eyes that you two are pretty damn fond of each other. As for you and me? Well, let's just say since you're my favorite patient and I've decided to be your favorite Doctor, we do pretty good ourselves. But just because we like you so much doesn't mean we're offering you charity, so we don't want you to get hung up on all of that. As a matter-of-fact, we'll be asking you for something in return. Actually two things, but Rachel doesn't care as much about the second one as I do, so I guess I'll be the only one asking that."

Daisy didn't respond right away, and when she turned her dubious sights on the hollow winter gray outside, Jack Lewen thought it best not to wait until she did. "Believe me, it's not that bad Daisy. All we're asking is that we be allowed to send you to community college while you're with us. And if we do, you gotta promise to study hard. That way, maybe in a year or so, you'll have your grades at a point where we can send you to UCLA with those friends of yours, Cora and Laney. Now I don't think I'd be exaggerating if I said it's something that'll probably do you a lot of good, but it's still something that's gonna take some effort on your part, so it's really up to you."

Whether it took a month, six, or even a year, didn't matter. What stirred inside Daisy was the mere suggestion, that at some point, Mansfield might actually become a distant memory... finally. And though she did her best to remain calm while absorbing the overwhelming possibility, even latching onto the windowsill in order to steady herself and appear that way, her head was pounding, her stomach was doing somersaults, and her chin was quivering because of the tugging on her heart.

"Now the second thing," Jack Lewen added, tongue-in-cheek, "the thing Rachel doesn't care about as much as I do, is that you never turn the stereo down when I'm playing a Beatles album. Especially The White Album. If you do, it'll only make me turn it up – louder than ever. So what do you say?" Jack Lewen asked, after a brief pause. "Think you can handle those two things?"

Before Daisy could answer, even though her answer was going to come in the form of a grateful, teary-eyed gaze, she needed a few moments to gather herself; which she spent by wiping away the window-fog created by her own harried breathing – smearing, in turn, what, for a lifetime running, had been a cold and grim view.

The two things Rachel Lewen liked best about spring were changing the window displays in her boutique (although it wasn't so much the new clothes, but the reminder they served that after months of depressing winter skies, summer was finally just around the corner), and planting flowers in her garden (a passion she picked up from her mother, and one she looked forward to sharing with Daisy Jo).

"Most of the stuff is already out back, but you might wanna grab another pair of gloves from the garage," she called out.

"Okay. I'll be down in a couple of secs," Daisy Jo called back from atop the stairs.

Rachel smiled, and then opened the french-doors that lead to the rolling twenty-acre backyard she and Jack purchased five years back, and stepped outside, where the warmth of the late April sun was tempered by the gentle breeze that washed over her shoulders. Still, with the busy sounds of spring breaking open all around her, Rachel felt it only fitting to take off her shoes and let her bare feet explore the intoxicating freshness of the dew-laden grass.

When the Lewens first built their house, the garden, though lovely, was little more than a colorful boundary for the cobblestone patio out back. Each spring, however, Rachel added to it, until finally, she had to hire a contractor to lay a cobblestone walkway just so she and Jack could meander through the middle of what had become a long and winding trail of splendor and tranquility.

Be that as it may, Daisy assumed the garden was no larger an area, and would take no more effort to work than the very garden her own mother was so fond of when she was alive. And then she joined Rachel outside and saw up close what the snow had been hiding these past months. "Wow, I had no idea it was so big. You don't get a real view of it from the house, ya know?"

Rachel nodded. "Yeah, I guess it is rather large for a garden… although every year it seems like there's still something else I can do to it."

"Well," Daisy quipped after a deliberate pause, "why don't you plant flowers across the full twenty acres. Then you'll be done with it once and for all."

Rachel slipped her sunglasses down to the bridge of her perfectly tapered nose, and squinted sharply. "Hmmm, not a bad idea. How are you at turning soil?"

"That depends... will it be just me crawlin' around on my hands and knees? Or will you be supplying a team of oxen and all the biscuits and gravy they can eat?"

Rachel did her best to keep a straight face, but that only lasted until Daisy lost control of her own, at which point they shared a short, but healthy laugh. It turned out to be the first of many. As a matter-of-fact, it wasn't until sometime after lunch, when Daisy said, "This may sound stupid, but I'm gonna ask anyway," that the conversation took its first obvious turn.

"What's that?" Rachel replied.

Daisy cupped her hands around the butt of the hoe and leaned her upper body against it. "Well, with so many flowers out here, how do you know what you want to plant? I mean, like with the colors and everything. How do you decide?"

Rachel straightened up, taking a few moments to roll the stiffness out of her neck before responding. "I don't really, Jo. I used to though. I used to think certain flowers or colors belonged with other flowers or colors – probably because that's the way my mother did it. Then one day... I don't know... I just decided flowers are flowers. The more the merrier. Seems more natural that way."

"Yeah, but like every year you start over. Do you pick the same stuff as the year before? I mean, how do ya know what you want to grow?"

"Well, for starters, a lot of the flowers are perennials. Tulips, daffodils, that sort of thing. They come up every year, so I don't think about those at all. After that, about the only flowers I know I'm going to plant more of are roses and daisies. Roses because I think they're so dignified looking – plus they smell good. And daisies... daisies because I think... I don't know, I guess because there's no other flower I'd rather see first thing in the morning. But that's it. That's all the thinking I put into it. Then again," Rachel added, as she tossed her gloves to the ground, "that's the real beauty of flowers. All you really need is dirt and water. If they're of a mind to grow, they'll do the rest. And since I've not seen too many ugly flowers in my life, it's pretty hard to screw up."

147

Daisy stabbed her toes at the grass, and then dipped her head to one side and let her gaze drift away from Rachel's. "Can I... can I ask you something else?"

"Don't be silly," Rachel replied, somewhat puzzled by the abrupt change in Daisy's demeanor. "You can ask me anything you want."

"Well then, if you like daisies so much, how come you make a habit of callin' me Jo?"

Rachel pondered the question, and then asked one of her own. "Why, do you not like it when I call you that?"

"It's not that I don't like it. It's just... it's just... I dunno," Daisy stammered, suddenly embarrassed she brought the matter up. "Let's just forget I even mentioned it."

Rachel remained silent until Daisy looked at her, whereupon she embraced her with a soft smile, and an equally soft tone of voice. "Jack and I sometimes call you Jo for the same reason we sometimes call you Daisy. Your mother gave two unique and very pretty names to one unique and very pretty girl. Believe it or not, we just use them both because we like them both. That's really all there is to it. But now you tell me – why are you bringing it up if it doesn't bother you?"

Daisy stabbed her toes at the grass again. "Because I thought you hated my first name."

"And you never said anything until now? Why?" Rachel asked.

"I dunno. You guys have been so good to me, I guess I just didn't want to make a big deal out of it."

"Ya know that's nonsense, don't you?"

"I know. The whole thing's stupid."

"That's not what I mean."

"What then?" Daisy asked, her befuddled expression barely able to fight through the screaming glare of the afternoon sun.

Rachel stood up and brushed the dirt from her pants. "C'mon, I'm kinda thirsty. Let's take a break."

Daisy agreed and followed Rachel to the patio, where she pulled off her gloves and sat down; her weary-stained sigh breaking in just as she leaned back in the chair and stretched her legs.

"I used to hate ice tea," Rachel announced as she took hold of the pitcher and proceeded to fill two glasses. "I used to think you had to drink it hot, or not at all. Then one night Jack and I were out to dinner and he talked me in to trying a Long Island Ice Tea. Of course one lead to two, two lead to one more than I should've had, and, well, the next thing I knew I was doing a striptease right there in the restaurant. Jack swears he pulled me out of there before I got too out of hand, but you know Jack. As soon as he starts laughing that devious little laugh of his, it's hard to know what to believe." Rachel snickered at the memory, and then remarked, "I've been a fan of ice tea ever since."

Daisy managed to look amused, though her expression only lasted the few seconds it took Rachel to finish her drink, at which point the little-girl grin curled up at the corners of her mouth eased back into the arms of a question she felt it necessary to repeat. "So then, what did you mean?"

Rachel took off her sunglasses and squared her shoulders toward her young and special friend. "What I meant," she replied, her brilliant hazel eyes doing their best to adjust to the sudden change in light, "had nothing to do with the subject matter. We could've been talking about the man on the moon and it wouldn't have mattered. It's the fact that you were actually hesitant, or better yet, even afraid to say something that was obviously troubling you. That's the nonsense part, because you shouldn't be."

"Maybe so," Daisy replied, "but try growin' up in my house and tell me that."

Rachel reached across the table and gently squeezed Daisy's hand, despite Daisy's natural tendency to curl her fingers and pull away. "Whether or not you know it, Jack and I have somewhat of an appreciation for where you came from. We understand more than you know."

Daisy smirked.

"Okay, so I'm not the first one to tell you that," Rachel conceded. "But that doesn't mean it's not true. The important thing is that you learn to forgive yourself for all the things that weren't your fault to begin with. Be it your mother's death, having to give your baby up for adoption, or being abused by your father. No matter what you think, none of those things could be helped."

"I'm aware of all that," Daisy replied, the words marching out of her mouth in agitated succession. "Unfortunately, leavin' that stuff behind is easier said than done."

Rachel nodded her head pensively, and then turned, and for the next several moments gazed beyond the shadows of her garden, across sweeping fields sewn together like tapestries of never-ending green, that otherwise measured the rolling boundaries of the place she'd come to know and love. "When Jack was growing up," she finally mused, "he had a younger brother named David. I never met him, but according to Jack he was really a nice kid. Cute too. Anyway, David looked up to Jack like it was his mission in life. The thing is, Jack had a wild streak, even for a kid. I mean, it was all very innocent... he just liked to see how far he could take something without getting into trouble for it. You know, pullin' pranks, practical jokes, that sort of thing. The problem was, anytime Jack did something David would try and outdo him. And then one day he did... and something happened.... something very bad." Rachel's cryptic setting no sooner fell into place when she abruptly turned toward Daisy, and declared, "Jack's father killed David. And Jack witnessed the whole thing."

"What?"

"You heard me right."

"No, I know, but why? I mean..."

"David evidently wanted to set a new standard," Rachel broke in, "so he decided to make his father the object of his little joke. He rigged the garage door so that it couldn't be opened; meaning when Saturday morning rolled around and his father was ready to leave for the office, he couldn't get out of the garage. Anyway, the long and short of it is that Jack's father wrestled with the door until he got it to work... or so he thought, because the moment he got in his car to leave, the door gave way. I mean it just sorta came crashing down, part of it landing on the car itself. Now according to Jack, his father had a scary temper, the kind that made you wanna run and hide whenever he got mad. Unfortunately David was laughing too hard to do either. Of course once his father got a hold of him the laughing stopped and the screaming started. It got so bad Jack raced down the stairs to find out what was going on, and just as he rushed into the room he saw his father throw David backwards – except instead of hitting the wall David lost his balance and fell down the basement stairs. He umm... he broke his neck and died instantly."

"Oh my god," Daisy gasped. "That's terrible."

Rachel shook her head. "I know, but that's not the end of it. Jack's father made Jack swear not to tell anyone. You know, we'll both get in a lot of trouble for it, so stick to the story that David was horsing around and fell down the stairs by accident, kind of thing. Meaning, don't tell the police, and don't tell your mother, who just happened to be in Pittsburgh at the time helping her sister with a new baby. So now you've got this twelve-year-old kid who's expected to endure the loss of his brother, what becomes his mother's nervous breakdown, his father's excessive drinking and depression, and perhaps, worst of all, the guilt of knowing what really happened. I mean we're talkin' about a kid who ends up closing himself off so completely, when he's not walking around like a deaf mute or throwing violent tantrums, he's in a psychiatrist's office explaining how he can't eat, can't sleep, wets the bed and cries for no reason at all. Anyway, about a year later Jack told his father he couldn't take it anymore – told him he didn't think he could keep quiet. Well… evidently his father wasn't ready to cope with the outcome of that, so later that day he went into the garage and shot himself in the head. Suffice it to say, Jack's nightmares were just beginning." Rachel inched back in her chair and gazed off into the distance once again, absorbing the words to a story she thought she'd never tell anyone.

Daisy too scanned the wide open fields, her eyes drifting aimlessly as she searched for something to say. Yet, there was only the sound of stunned silence – thick and unsettling it dissipated only when Rachel took it upon herself to continue. "He went to live with his aunt and uncle," she said, her words clothed in a haze of reflection. "The same aunt his mother was visiting in Pittsburgh. That's what first gave Jack the push he needed. That's what gave him the chance to start new. I was around back then too," she added, the creases around her eyes deepening as she broke into a heartfelt smile. "My family lived next door to them. Jack was a handful all right – all the way through high school. But it didn't matter. I saw so much good in him, I fell hopelessly in love with him anyway."

Daisy wiped away the tears sitting in her eyes. "Listen, I'm really sorry for the way I sounded before. I had no idea."

"I know," Rachel replied, "but there's no way you would. It's not something Jack or I would ever tell you. It's not something we would normally tell anyone."

"Well, if it means anything, I'm glad you did."

"If it helps you learn to trust yourself… or trust the fact that you can recover from your past then so am I. Just remember, sometimes you have to learn to trust other people so they can help you too."

Daisy stretched her arm across the table and gathered Rachel's hand in her own.

Charlie Bridger couldn't get over it. Here, only yesterday, Martin Starr, Reverend Martin Starr, was tellin' him that he ain't seen hide nor hair of Daisy in longer than he could remember – "Ain't even heard a single word about her" – when out of the blue, standing at a traffic light not fifty feet away, there she was. All gussied up too. Like she just stepped out of the pages of one of those fancy girl magazines, or somethin'.

But Charlie wasn't of a mind to run off and give Martin the news. Not just yet, anyway. Especially since Martin would probably start preachin' how Daisy's pregnancy wasn't just a condemnable sin, but one tantamount to the blasphemy of... Charlie scratched the back of his head... well, somethin' somebody would consider blasphemous, at any rate.

And it wouldn't stop there, Charlie thought, still scratching the back of his head. Heck no. Martin would likely take a slug or two of whiskey, curl his upper lip as if he hated the taste of the very thing he couldn't get enough of, and then start railing on about how he single-handedly preserved the sanctity of his house simply by throwin' Daisy's pregnant ass out of it before she had a chance to return with a cuddly, little bundle of condemnable baby. It was the kind of ranting and raving Charlie had to be ready for, 'cuz he found it awfully tiring on the ears. It didn't matter if Charlie agreed with it neither. Fact is even if he did, he wouldn't voice his opinion on the subject for fear it would just give Martin the ammunition he needed to launch into another such tirade.

What Charlie found even more tiring, however, was trying to figure out why? Why, after months and months on end, was Martin still poppin' off about it – carryin' on like there was no tomorrow? Was it all because Daisy Jo let herself get pregnant, not only spoilin' the good name Martin gave her, but spoilin' his good name too? Was it because Martin had grown so comfortable with being waited on hand and foot, that despite his constant bellyachin' about Daisy spendin' many a day refusin' his more personal advances, he still missed havin' her around? 'Course, if that were the case then maybe the only thing Martin was really missin' was somebody to smack around whenever the smackin' mood took hold...

Or was it, Charlie suddenly wondered, as he slipped around the corner, having turned it up a notch just to keep Daisy's spirited pace in view, because Daisy, as destitute as she mighta been with that full belly and all, never got on her hands and knees and begged to come back home? Maybe, just maybe, by not sayin' a damn thing to her daddy, Daisy found an interestin' way to get in the last word – somethin' Martin's been havin' a hard time with ever since.

Whatever the reason, one thing was certain, Charlie concluded – Daisy Jo Starr was a mighty fine lookin' thing. A mighty fine lookin' thing indeed. In fact, Charlie's eyes were so busy racing up and down her backside, it wasn't until she climbed into some strange car ten minutes later that he looked at his watch and realized just how long he'd actually been following her. But he did take note of the location. And he did return the next two days to watch Daisy disappear inside that same strange car again.

The third day, now that was a different story altogether. On the third day Charlie brought along his pickup truck so he could see for himself just where n' the hell Daisy and the strange car were headin' off to.

Three stoplights, a handful of miles, and some twenty minutes later, he found out too. And wouldn't you know it, about all Charlie could do was fashion himself a jaw-droppin', eye-poppin' shake of the head.

Martin Starr, Reverend Martin Starr, swayed back and forth, beer in one hand, bourbon in the other, and waited for good ol' Charlie Bridger to open the garage door. Yet, since Martin had been drinking at a steady clip for the past couple of hours, once Charlie wiped the grease from his hands and yanked on the rope that set the sectional door in motion, he couldn't propel himself forward anyway; his efforts resembling little more than a bad imitation of a high-wire circus act.

"Say Rev," Charlie called out with a laugh, his friend's inability to figure out the difference between north and south proving to be the funniest thing he'd seen since the last time Martin's legs struggled with the notion, "if ya ain't figured it out by now, the door's this-a-way."

Martin steadied himself as best he could, looked at Charlie, and snapped, "Fool? Who you callin' fool?"

"What the hell you talkin' 'bout?" Charlie shot back with a look of disbelief. "I didn't call you no fool!"

"Cuz if you wanna see a fool Charlie, alls ya need to do is have yourself a little looksie in the mirror," Martin continued, his sardonic grin about as cockeyed as his walk.

Charlie drifted a couple of steps closer to the two empty car-bays and gave Martin and his suggestion the once over. Still, not the least bit interested in pursuing an argument that would only prove to be a futile effort, he opted for quiet, figurin' it was only a matter of time before the liquor changed Martin's direction once again anyway.

Of course Charlie had no way of knowing what that direction might be. And even if he did, he certainly wasn't expecting it to lead Martin to the front of the filling station, where he dropped his drawers to take a leak at the precise moment The Jaye women, Fay and her daughter Gay, pulled in and honked for service.

Nevertheless, Charlie waited until his friend and partner appeared to be flappin' out the last few drops before walking out of the garage. "Don't get it caught," he snickered, as he strolled by him.

"Catchin' it ain't the problem Charlie. It's whether this zipper has enough gumption to keep Mr. Big Dick locked up," Martin replied, his smile proudly stretched from ear to ear.

Charlie did his best to keep from bustin' a gut, but the moment he approached the car, and said, "Afternoon ma'am... filler up?" he helped himself to another eyeful of Martin and ended up cuttin' loose with a grandiose mixture of mouth spray and laughter; the laughter falling harmlessly about, the mouth spray falling not so harmlessly about Fay Jaye's face.

"Why you no good dirty son-of-a-bitch!" She barked.

Charlie quickly sucked in all the laughter he could, though a trifle still managed to slip out before he apologized.

"Never mind that!" Fay Jaye barked again. "Just gimmee somethin' to wipe my face with!"

"Why, yes ma'am. Sure thing." Charlie reached in the back pocket of his coveralls and pulled out an oil-spotted rag. "Don't mind the looks of it. It's clean dirt. Hell, I cleaned the doggone thing just a few days ago myself."

Fay Jaye dismissed Charlie's suggestion with a brusque wave of the hand, and then grabbed hold of her daughter's arm and used her shirtsleeve to dry her fleshy cheeks. "Lucky for you this stinkin' car of mine's bone-dry," she chided, pushing her daughter's arm away. "Otherwise, I'd be lookin' to take my business somewheres else."

"Yes ma'am, I'm sure you would. Now how 'bout I filler-up for ya?"

"Like I said, I'm bone-dry. Just make sure that damn fool stays away from me."

Charlie glanced in the direction of Martin, decided he was far more interested in drinking than he was in wandering over to the car, and then lowered his body until his head was just about sticking through the open window. "Why sure ma'am, I'll protect ya," he responded with the sincerity of a man who enjoys ringing sarcasm from his tongue. "But tell me somethin' first. What's the girl's name? Heck, she's a pretty little thing. What's your name child?"

"Gay Jaye."

"Well Gay Jaye, my name's Charlie Bridger, and you can come visit me anytime you want. You hear? You and your mama both." Charlie thought about reaching in the car to shake hands with his pretty new friend, but the sharp glare pouring out of her mother's eyes convinced him otherwise. As such, he simply tipped his head, and said, "I'll be gettin' your gas now ma'am. But don't you hesitate none about comin' back for a visit. Ya hear?"

156

Fay Jaye shook her head and winced. "Just filler-up so I can get the hell outta here. Okay?"

"Yes ma'am. Right away."

In between polishing off one beer and thinking about having another, Martin watched Charlie shuffle from pumping gas to cleaning the car windshield. But when it came to making change, he was on his feet, counting what he couldn't see. And the moment Fay Jaye pealed away in her car, his pockets were ready for filling.

"Ya think you can wait long enough for me to put it in the register?" Charlie asked, while making his way into the garage. "Besides, we're only talkin' about ten bucks. It ain't like you'd be missin' out on a whole lot even if I was of a mind to hold out on you... which I ain't."

"Says you," Martin countered.

"Yeah, so?"

Martin set his can of beer on the chewed-up, tool-littered workbench and folded his arms. "Are you sayin' ya never held out on me before Charlie?"

"Yep. That's what I'm saying."

"Well now, how do I know that for sure?"

Charlie ran his greasy fingers through his patchy head of greasy hair, and sneered mischievously. "I guess you'll just have to take my word for it. Same as I gotta take yours."

"What if I don't wanna take your word for it? What then? And what the hell is so goddamn funny?"

Charlie didn't have to look at Martin long to know his eyes were turning as cold and hard as the words coming out of his mouth. Of course, one mention of Daisy's whereabouts would change everything. The drunk talk, the fightin' look, everything. The fact that Charlie might even get away with stuffin' the ten bucks in his pocket didn't hurt matters either. Still, Charlie wasn't certain if this was the best time and place to break the news. He faced the same question about a week ago and decided against it, figuring he'd run into a more opportune moment... like now. Yet, might there be an even better day lurking on the horizon? Yes? No? Maybe?

It was only when Martin unfolded his arms, took a step closer to him, and asked again what was so funny, that Charlie decided.

22

The white picket fence extended well beyond the front of the house, though like a shadow, at no time was it any more than a wistful decoration – forgotten after a single glance, dismissed like a mistaken knock at the door, it stood prisoner to the harsh realities of the seasons, spared only because it received a fresh coat of paint every couple of years or so.

Somewhere along the way, however, Daisy came to recognize it as something more. The perimeter of calm, it surrounded, embodied and marked a warm path to the Lewen household, where, once inside, the strains of another nonstop day of school and work melted from the comfort within. "Anybody home?" She called out.

There was no answer, and Daisy didn't really expect one, Wednesday being the one day of the week when she'd usually get home before Rachel and Jack; which was all just as well since it gave her a chance to get dinner started (something she did every chance she could, despite Jack's light-hearted claims that she was trying to poison him).

With the spring and summer semesters under her belt, and the fall term a month from winding up, Daisy was more at ease now than at anytime in recent memory; her solid grades providing a certain measure of confidence at school, Rachel and Jack providing a constant measure of hope in just about everything else. Still, there were moments when Daisy's past hovered near, when ugly visions of her father stirred, only to slip into delicate thoughts of her mother, or the baby she let get away. And though such thoughts often lingered, they no longer overwhelmed her like in days gone by.

But that was before today – before black skies descended and a crisp November wind settled in – before the branches of barren trees shivered and their once proud and colorful leaves gathered on the ground like dust – before Charlie Bridger turned onto the gravel-filled road, pointed at whatever lay beyond the hood of his pickup truck, and said, "The Jew bastard's house is another couple-a-hundred yards up ahead."

"You sure Charlie, 'cuz I sure as hell don't see no kinda house nowhere."

"Hell yeah," flew Charlie's hard-boiled reply. "Ya see this big ol' long fence here? Well now, all of that... I mean to tell ya, all of that belongs to that son-of-a-bitchin' Jew queer she lives with. The reason ya can't see his house – now that's 'cuz it happens to sit around the corner apiece."

Martin turned his head to grab another look at what they had already passed. "It's a damn good thing we didn't come by here till I sobered up some. Otherwise with this darkness and all, I ain't sure I woulda been able to see much of anything. Hell, I can't hardly see nothin' now. How much property ya figure ol' Jew-boy's got?"

"Dunno, but it's some kinda property all right," Charlie conceded. "A helluva lot more than any stinkin' Jew should have. Then again, any amount is too much for a Jew. Don't you think so?"

Martin Starr, Reverend Martin Starr, didn't respond until Charlie eased his truck to a stop and the setting of a big white house unfolded. "Goddamn right I think so," he spewed. "I'll tell ya somethin' else I think too."

"What's that?"

Martin reached for the pint of bourbon buried under his seat. "I think Jews and natural whores is all alike."

Charlie tilted his head like a confused and mangy puppy-dog. "What the hell you mean a natural whore?"

"C'mon now Charlie, you know what I'm talkin' about. A natural whore... the kind of woman that's born corrupted."

"Meanin' what, she's born with some bad blood? And before ya answer Martin, I gotta tell ya, for me that bad blood is what make's 'em so damn entertainin'."

Martin rolled his neck and shoulders around, limbering up for the nice big slug of whiskey he was about to take. "I ain't sayin' whores ain't entertainin' Charlie. Lord knows I find 'em entertainin' myself. But that's why he put them kinda women on this here earth... to entertain men like me n' you. The thing I'm sayin' is that if a woman ain't born a natural whore, she might be turned into one, but it ain't natural. Meanin', she wasn't born corrupted, someone made her that way. See the difference?"

"I hear what you're sayin'. I just ain't sure what you're gettin' at."

Martin wiped the whiskey from the corners of his mouth and handed the bottle to his best and only drinking buddy. "What I'm gettin' at is that this ol' Jew-boy, he turned Daisy into some kinda

159

whore. Ain't no other way to say it. The good Lord knows she weren't born that way. And I sure as hell didn't raise her up that way." Martin flashed Charlie an open palm. "And before you go gettin' ahead of yourself, don't think her gettin' pregnant makes her a whore neither. That was just a piece of bad luck, that's all that was."

Charlie took on the look of a confused and mangy puppy-dog again. "Well, now, how come you wasn't thinkin' that way back when she was carryin' the seed?"

"B'cuz back then it came up on me at a bad time. I mean, if I didn't have nothin' else to be concerned about, my preachin' and whatnot, then I believe I mighta been able to process the information a little differently. Unfortunately Daisy saw fit to dump that news in my lap without regard to my situation, forcin' my hand, if you will. 'Course, that was sometime ago, so discussin' that garbage now don't make no sense. But that don't mean I gotta stand back while some Jew-boy is turnin' her into a whore. Hell no. That much I figure I can rectify."

Charlie threw his eyebrows skyward and for a brief moment his beady brown eyes appeared big and round. "I dunno Martin," he proffered. "Looks to me like she mighta already rectified the situation herself."

"Listen Charlie, if there's any rectifyin' to do, I'll be the one doin' it. Ya hear?"

"I didn't say you wasn't gonna do it Rev. I'm just sorta wonderin' why and how, that's all."

"How? You wanna know how?" Martin returned, reaching for the bottle of bourbon once it appeared Charlie wasn't interested in giving it back. "Hell, that's easy. I'm gonna take her home and turn her away from these whorin' ways of hers. It ain't too late ya know."

"But who's the rectifyin' really for Rev… you or her?" Charlie asked, the moment he lost control of the bottle.

"Whataya mean Charlie. I ain't been nothin' but charitable my whole entire life. So I'm doin' it for her, naturally."

Charlie ignored the whiskey-burn taking root in his belly and cracked a wry grin. "Then you ain't expectin' her to put up much of a stink, are ya Mr. Charity?"

Martin nodded his head until he finished swallowin' a mouthful of firewater, whereupon he grimaced, burped, and said, "First off, I know you're just funnin' me Charlie boy, so I ain't takin' no offense.

Secondly, I do expect some kinda ruckus outta Daisy. But that's b'cuz she never did know what was best for her own self. The thing is, she can do all the kickin' and screamin' she wants. It still won't matter none. I'm gonna see to it she turns her back on these whorin' ways, one way or the other."

"Yeah? Well whataya aimin' to do if the Jew bastard's home?"

"Why, ya think he is?"

"Goddamn Martin, look at his house. It ain't lit up like a Christmas tree 'cuz it's empty. Besides that, it's after nine. Where else is he gonna go around here?"

"Yeah, I 'spose you're right. 'Course seein' as how history's taught us that Jews prefer runnin' over fightin', I don't figure it'll matter even if he is."

"So then what, ya just gonna march up there, knock on the door and take hold of her?"

"Yep. And if Mr. Jew-boy don't like it then maybe I'll do a little knockin' on his head too." And with those words firmly tucked away, Martin took one last gulp of whiskey, deposited the bottle in Charlie's hand, and hopped out of the truck.

Charlie waited for the door to slam shut, and then jiggled the pint of bourbon, and mumbled, "Mr. Charity my ass." Nevertheless, he quickly sucked down whatever was left and joined Martin in his benevolent quest up the drive.

From a distance the front door looked like an obscure figure, lost amid a penetrating darkness where restless shadows danced beyond the reach of the moon's subtle glare. Yet, once Martin and Charlie reached the porch its body came into view, and silhouetted by the restrained beauty of etched glass, it was easily the finest looking door either of them had ever seen, prompting Charlie to mutter, "That sure is a fancy lookin' mother-scratcher. Wonder how she knocks?"

"Probably like a fuckin' door," Martin replied, his tone a combination of pop and sizzle. "Only I'm gonna be the one findin' out b'cuz you're gonna be standin' off to the side there."

"Just in case ol' Jew-boy's more than you can handle, eh?" Charlie countered, his sarcasm as plain as the night.

"Make all the fun you want Charlie. I just wanna make sure we're ready for him in case we need to be."

"Hell Rev, let him put up a stink if he wants," Charlie proposed, his fingers skimming the door's sleek oak finish. "Legally I don't

161

figure there's much he can do about you stealin' back your own daughter... even if you were the one to throw her out in the first place. And physically... well now, if he wants to give it a whirl, let's let him."

"I aim to," Martin said, shooing Charlie away. "Just as soon as you quit yappin' and get where I told ya."

"Yes sir Captain Rev. Whatever you say Sir."

Martin ignored Charlie and his acrimonious five-star salute, stationed himself front and center, and gave the front door a couple of solid whacks, the sting in his palm settling only after the door opened and Rachel Lewen appeared.

"Yes? May I help you?"

"Name's Martin Starr," Martin announced imperiously. "Reverend Martin Starr. I've come for my daughter."

Rachel did her best to remain calm, although she couldn't escape the unexpected chill that for a staggering moment weakened her knees and fastened a look of trepidation in her eyes.

"Said my name's Martin Starr, Reverend Martin Starr. And I've come for my daughter."

"I heard you. So?"

"So if ya heard me then how 'bout bein' a good little gal and go fetch her for me."

Rachel shook her head slowly, deliberately, and replied in a voice as tight and rigid as her hold on the doorknob, "She's not here. Now how 'bout you bein' a good little boy and get the hell out of here before I call the police."

Martin folded his arms across his puffy chest and took a step closer to the doorway. "Yeah, well guess what? I don't believe a thing you're tellin' me."

"Yeah, well that would be too bad except I don't really care what you believe," Rachel shot back. "Now get off my property before I call the police."

"Sure thing," Martin spewed, his dark eyes dancing back and forth in an effort to see beyond the foyer. "Just as soon as I have a little look for myself."

"I don't think so," Rachel insisted.

Martin leaned forward, inflated chest, smirk and all, and said, "Oh Yeah? Well now how's a pretty little gal like you proposin' to stop a man like me?"

"With this," Jack Lewen proclaimed as he came up behind Charlie Bridger, his father's old Browning rifle resting snuggly against his shoulder. "She's proposin' to stop you with this."

"Whoa, whoa, whoa – hold on there ace," Charlie pleaded, quickly back peddling from out the same eerie darkness from which Jack so unexpectedly appeared. "I ain't no part of this. Came along for the ride, that's all I did."

Jack waved the gun-barrel in the direction of the road. "Then I guess you'll want to be part of the ride home too, won't ya?"

"Oh yeah. You betcha I do. You betcha." Charlie replied, the words flying out of his mouth faster than they ever flew before.

"Now hold on there Charlie, you ain't goin' nowhere," Martin instructed. "We come for my daughter, and we ain't leavin' till I get her."

Charlie glanced at Martin, and then back at Jack, before launching his arms high in the air. "Hold on nothin' Martin. This ol' boy looks like he means it. And even if he don't, that gun of his does."

Jack snickered. "So your name's Charlie, eh? Well now Charlie, you like the ladies?"

"What?"

"I said the ladies, Charlie, the ladies. Because if you like 'em and you wanna make sure you can still go dancin' with 'em with both balls attached, then I suggest you take everything I say very seriously. I also suggest that your friend there has the good sense to get off the porch." Jack carefully pivoted and steadied his aim at Martin. "And unless you think you're Superman, I suggest you be quick about it."

With his arms waving and fingers pointing like he was in the throes of a fire and brimstone Sunday, Martin moved away from the door, and bellowed, "Now wait just a goddamn minute! My name's Martin Starr, Reverend Martin Starr, and I come for my daughter! Now I ain't sure just who n' the hell you think you are, but lemme tell ya, without that rifle I wouldn't be gettin' off nothin', much less leavin' this place without Daisy. Fact is, without that rifle, I don't figure you for much at all."

"I guess that means it's a good thing I have it then, doesn't it Mr. Starr?"

"Reverend Starr. I said Reverend Starr. Now maybe bein' a Jew don't mean much to you, but bein' a Reverend means I at least expect to be referred to as such."

"And I said be quick about it. Now maybe you have a hard time understanding things, but that means I expect you to be standing next to your buddy Charlie within the next five seconds, or praying for some divine intervention." Jack spread his legs evenly to balance his weight, cocked his rifle, in turn cracking open the still night air with the sound of the gun's ominous threat, and asked, "Get my drift?"

"Don't… don't get all… don't get all hasty now… I'm movin', see, I'm movin'," Martin said, the words bouncing off his tongue as quickly and calmly as his pounding heart and dancing feet would allow. "I'm movin'."

"Don't worry Mr. Starr, I don't get hasty. I just get mad when I'm forced to be in the company of such profound ignorance," Jack stated, his heedful pace slowly carrying him up the porch steps where he handed the rifle to his wife and watched her disappear inside the house.

Martin eyeballed Charlie before letting his bewildered sights fall back on Jack Lewen. "You callin' me stupid? Is that what you're doin'?"

"No," Jack quipped, his shadow growing taller the closer he moved toward the front yard. "I'm actually calling both of you stupid."

"Well now, for a little man like you to give up control of his gun and then tell two other men like us they're stupid… well, I guess it makes ya kinda wonder just who the hell the stupid one is. Don't it?" Martin queried with a laugh.

"On the contrary," Jack returned. "In fact, the gun wasn't even loaded. I only brought it out with me because it seemed like the easiest way to get you to do what I wanted."

Martin took a quick look at the house.

"If you're looking for Daisy, she's probably heading upstairs with my wife and some popcorn so they can watch the festivities – just in case I decide to kick the hell out of the two of you."

"Somethin' you figure you can do, eh smart-guy?" Charlie snarled, his sense of bravado humming along at full throttle once again.

"Yes Charlie, it's somethin' I figure I can do. Although I don't have to. Instead you two morons can go on about your business in peace and Daisy can just swear her complaint out tomorrow."

"Complaint? What the hell you talkin' 'bout, complaint?" Martin barked, his focus no longer on scanning the windows to catch a glimpse of Daisy.

"Complaint, you know, for having beaten and raped your daughter far too many times to count. That kind of complaint."

Martin jabbed his finger at the hollow darkness. "Now you listen to me you little stinkin' son-of-a-bitch..."

"No, Mr. Starr, you listen to me," Jack ordered, his own finger taking on the look of an exclamation point. "Tomorrow morning Daisy is gonna visit the prosecutor's office. She's wanted to do it for months, but I talked her out of it. Told her as long as you didn't bother her, she should leave well enough alone and get on with her life. She did, but now you went ahead and fucked it all up. That's because I promised to do it her way the moment you reared up that insane little head of yours. And since I never, ever break a promise... you're shit-out-of-luck!"

"Oh yeah? Well who do you suppose is gonna believe a whorin' little gal like Daisy after all this time anyway?"

"Frankly it doesn't matter Mr. Starr. The prosecutor and I have been best friends for longer than I can remember and he's gonna hound you just for the fun of making your life a living hell. You understand what I'm saying? Or you need me to spell it out for you?"

Martin wiped the back of his neck that despite the November chill was growing moist with sweat. "Yeah? Well ya know what I think? I think you ain't nothin' but a stinkin' little dirty Jew. You understand what I'm sayin'? Or ya need me to spell stinkin' little dirty Jew for ya?"

In all the years Jack Lewen had been studying karate, either as a student, or teacher, there were only a handful of instances when his anger catapulted out of control. The first few times occurred soon after his father's suicide – after the dignity of karate unveiled itself, but before its teachings of respect and self-discipline could harness his inner rage and confusion. Beyond that, however, it wasn't until he and Rachel were accosted by two knife-wielding, wild-eyed looking derelicts during a weekend trip to New York several years later. And only then because they spit in Rachel's face after she refused to give up her purse. The entire episode ended within seconds, but Jack never forgot the indignation that unleashed his fury.

Similar, it was, to the indignation he was now feeling after Martin Starr, Reverend Martin Starr, called him a dirty Jew.

Similar too, it was, to the way Jack spun around and planted his foot in the side of Martin's face.

Martin went down in a heap, and though he initially tried to pull himself up, it wasn't until Jack dropped Charlie with the same move in the opposite direction that he was able to.

Of course, by then, Jack was bouncing up and down on the balls of his feet, waiting for Martin to make a move. Yet, when all Martin could come up with was a face-leading charge, Jack promptly reeled off a stinging flurry of right and left hand combinations; purposely holding back on the good stuff, however, until Martin was clearly wavering between falling face-up and landing facedown. At that point, Jack twirled around one last time and delivered the kind of explosion that kept Martin talking to himself, and Charlie huddled against a tree in fear until the police arrived.

"So… you umm, you all packed up?" Rachel asked as she walked into the bedroom, her tone a fragile mix of anguish and calm.

"Yes," Daisy replied, the snow outside now gathering on the very flower garden that only months ago she helped plant, and only moments ago she imagined coming back to life – perhaps to greet her like it had so many times before – perhaps to say goodbye for what may well be the very last time.

"Excited?"

Daisy wiped the tears sneaking into her endearing blue eyes, and then slowly turned and faced Rachel. "I'm gonna miss you," she whispered, the cracking in her soft voice evident nonetheless. "You've done so much for me… more than I could have ever imagined. I don't… I don't know how I can ever repay you."

Rachel's bittersweet smile faded as she neared the window, where she took hold of Daisy's outstretched hands, and whispered back, "We're gonna miss you too. I'm gonna miss you." And as her fingers twisted snuggly with Daisy's, she hung her head and quietly wept.

"You're the best… the best thing…" Daisy's quivering voice suddenly broke off and she grabbed hold of Rachel, hugging her tighter than she'd ever hugged anyone in her entire life. "I love you," she cried. "I love you."

"I love you too honey. I love you too."

It was another twenty minutes before Rachel and Daisy made their way down the stairs, and still, Jack was nowhere around, shuffling instead from room to room in search of something to do. A simple chore, a magazine to scan, unfinished paperwork for the hospital – anything to keep busy, anything to keep his mind off the simple fact that Daisy was leaving for California… today – moving to a place where Martin Starr, Reverend Martin Starr, was certain to never find her again – joining her two best friends, Cora and Laney… finally – starting the life that she'd been dreaming about since… well, since he's known her.

And yet, with the hope of Daisy's tomorrow set to sail, and the promise of a new life shimmering before her like the vast ocean she would soon see, all Jack could feel, for himself, for Rachel, were the serrated teeth of sadness and pain.

Still, and through it all, Jack did his best to remain composed. In fact, it was only when the taxi arrived and he knew it was time to say goodbye that those very efforts started to wane. "So, your friends know you're comin' right?" He asked, his eyes drifting back and forth between Daisy's radiant youth and the cold concrete driveway underneath him.

Daisy smiled. "For the tenth time, yes. Laney's picking me up from the airport at four. Cora's working so I won't see her till later."

"And you have the number of my buddy and his wife right... case you need anything? And don't be afraid to call them. They're expecting you, okay? And don't be afraid to call us too. Be it for money, or anything. Come to think of it, for Rachel's sake maybe you should even plan on calling a couple of times a week. And let me know what happens with school. One term at that community college, two at the most and you should be all set with UCLA. Just keep up all the good work you started here, okay? And don't forget to take time for yourself. Go to the beach, check out the mountains. And if you're ever feeling lonely just put on a Beatles album and think of me, okay? And don't forget..."

Daisy suddenly lunged forward, forcing Jack to catch her embrace. "I love you," she cried. "I'm gonna miss you."

Jack closed his eyes and hugged Daisy back with everything he had. "I love you too," he lamented, the cold winter air not quite enough to slow the stream of tears that followed. "I love you too."

The white picket fence extended well beyond the front of the house, and though its long and winding body soon disappeared from view, for Daisy, it would forever stand as a hallmark to a special place.

The Light of My Being

In this body
The silent weight of desperation
In these eyes
Black coals on a fiery night
In this face
A token stain of a man deeply scarred
But in this heart
I may know the light of my being

In these hands
I seize treasure, oft beguiled
In these arms
I hold restraint for that which I want to be
On my head
Rest's a crown of tempered thorns
But in this heart
I may know the light of my being

Of pride and glory
I balance the serrated road of chance
Of bounty immeasurable
I celebrate the perception of my spoils
Of time and turmoil
I swallow the anguish of an aging soul
But of this heart
I may know the light of my being

Of pomp and circumstance
I play along like a clown
Of dignity's grace
I stand alone, off to the side
Of pride and impudence
I've been lost between
But of this heart
I may know the light of my being

Of truth or consequence
I've retreated willfully
Of lies and candor
I've suffered casualties in full
Of compassion and vengeance
I've tasted the sin of weakness
But of this heart
I may know the light of my being

Of trust and treason
I salute the covenants of neither
Of freedom never-ending
I pledge it only to myself
Of god and country
I stand out like an island
But of this heart
I may know the light of my being

Of will and destiny
I walk narrow streets going nowhere
Of friends everlasting
I break bread with the still of seclusion
Of photographs and memories
I reflect on the moment
But of this heart
I may know the light of my being

Of legacies and donations
I bequeath to no one
Of misdeeds and transgressions
I am tempted more than not
Of opportunities knocking
I take them for granted
But of this heart
I may know the light of my being

Of common courtesy
I take pains not to waste it
Of common sense

Only that it makes sense to me
Of common valor
I remain a spectator
But of this heart
I may know the light of my being

Of velocity and change
I hang on for dear life
Of hopes and dreams
I watch them dance nearby
Of Avalon landings
I am lost at sea
But of this heart
I may know the light of my being

Of pain and fear
I pretend not to notice
Of love and hate
I have been torched by the fire they breathe
Of life and death
I stand aside while they chase each other
But of this heart
I may know the light of my being

In this body
Seeds of life not watered
In these eyes
Sterile lights on a barren night
In this face
Shadows of a man unbroken
But in this heart
I may know the light of my being

In these hands
I take stock of all others
In these arms
I embrace only myself
In my mind
I have visions of a man for all seasons

171

But in this heart
I may know the light of my being

About The Author

Author of the thriller, *The Lizard and the Fly*, as well as coauthor of the soon to be released, *About Face*, Robert Edward Levin resides in Michigan where he is currently working on his third novel. *The Glass Heart* is his first collection of short stories.

Printed in the United States
5207